L.D.P. San

Destroyer of Worlds

Alpha Ship One, Book two

Text © 2016 by Luis Samways

All rights reserved.

Cover Design by The Purple Book Co.

Luis Samways has asserted his right under the Copyright, Designs and Patents Act 1988 to be identified as the author of this work.

This book is a work of fiction and, except in the case of historical fact, any resemblance to actual persons, living or dead, is purely coincidental.

eBook edition first published in July 2016

Paperback edition first published in July 2016

******

V1.0

For more information on books by Luis Samways Visit:

www.LuisSamways.com

www.Twitter.com/LuisSamways

© 2016 by the Purple Book Co.

Table of Contents

L.D.P. Samways 1

Prologue 8

Chapter One 11

Chapter Two 17

"Flynn, I'm over…" 23

EARTH. MARINE DEPLOYMENT CENTER. NEVADA. OLD USA. 18.27 HOURS. 28

Chapter Three 35

Chapter Four 51

"Target locked – firing…" 55

Chapter Five 61

Chapter Six 80

Chapter Seven 96

Chapter Eight 106

The mission is a go. Ship inbound. Awaiting distraction. ETA one hour. 128

Chapter Nine 129

Chapter Ten 139

Chapter Eleven 151

Chapter Twelve 168

Chapter Thirteen 179

To Be Continued… 193

Sample 195

Prologue

"Every action, has a reaction," Commander Korr of the Annex Rebel Fleet said as he gazed upon his ever-faithful crew. The many faces that stared back at him forced the crook of his mouth to rise slightly. It made him smile to know that he had such a vast crew. A vast crew on an equally vast ship. A ship that stretched on for miles and miles. Hurtling through space toward its ever nearing objective. An objective that his people, the Annex people, wanted retribution on. And they would get their retribution. Korr was certain of it.

"And with every reaction to an action, comes a greater action. We have to be prepared for the worst. We don't know what's waiting for us out there, but we can assume that whatever it is; is bad. So bad that they sent us," the Commander said as he stood on the bridge of the large ship.

His loyal workforce stood below him, on a lowered steel platform. Some of them were dressed in military fatigues. While some were dressed in ship maintenance uniforms, covered in oil and dirt. Others wore normal clothing. Clean clothing. But one thing remained true regarding all of the people on his ship; they were mad. Angry. Seething. Vengeful. Violent. And impatient.

An unjust act had been committed. And it had to be answered with a just reply. Korr and his crew were that reply. A reply that would echo through the vacuum of space until many years passed, and nothing but the legend of what they had accomplished remained. But that was a long way off from where Korr and his crew were heading. They weren't interested in the legend of what they were about to do. All they were preoccupied with was making sure that justice was served, and it was served as quickly, and efficiently as possible.

"They say that everybody has their day," Commander Korr said as he began to pace the width of the bridge. His heavy boots clunked against the metal floor beneath him. "And our day is today," he continued.

"A day that has been lying in the wake of the atrocity committed by Earth and its people. An atrocity that the rest of the Galaxy let happen. They may stand idly by and do nothing, but we will not," the Commander said as he stopped pacing and raised his chin up. He stared at his people and stiffened his shoulders.

"For far too long, the people of Earth have gotten away with murder. They have gotten away with theft. And now they have gotten away with planet-wide genocide. A whole race gone. And for what? Greed? Envy? Lust?" the Commander said to a smatter of rumbling from his on-looking crew.

"The people of Earth may be our ancestors. They may share the same blood as us. They may even look a lot like us. But they aren't us. Somewhere down the line, they lost their way. They became what they feared. And what they feared since the dawn of man was evil. And quite frankly, that's all I see in them now. It's an evil that must be eradicated. An evil that must be answered to, or the very existence of us as a species will be compromised, solely based on the misguided actions of one sector of our species."

The many crewman and women being addressed by the Commander burst out into a roar of approval. They hollered loudly in agreement with their war chief. Their Commander. Their savior. Commander Korr nodded his head and broke out into a smile. His pearly white teeth shone as he stared at his subjects. He raised his left arm up and made a fist. The crewman and women below him fell silent, almost immediately.

"Every action…has a reaction…and this is ours," he snarled.

Chapter One

"No, no, no, no, no! You're doing it wrong!" Teresa said as she grabbed both of my arms and straightened them out. "You need to hold it like this," she continued, steadying my grip on the sword I was holding.

The both of us were dressed in fencing gear. We were aboard Sector Eight, a space station that orbited Earth. People stationed on Sector Eight usually spent most of their days goofing around, drinking beer and playing games. It was what the brass referred to as the *"cooling off"* station. It was a place where people scarred by the horrors of war could go and unwind.

The thing is, neither me nor Teresa were scarred by war. We were just dog tired. We'd spent three weeks on an alien planet, locked in a prison cell and were then forced to shuttle a nuclear bomb back to Earth, with the mission directive of destroying Earth with that bomb. Luckily, things had played out a little differently. We'd managed to turn things around and destroyed the alien threat that was making gains on our planet. My crew, or what was left of it, were all welcomed back like heroes. We'd done the unthinkable. We'd singlehandedly destroyed the majority of an alien species as it trudged its way toward Earth. We obliterated their convoy of warships and set off a chain reaction of explosions that was apparently felt hundreds of light years away! It was quite an achievement, but it wasn't an achievement I was particularly proud of.

Since we'd come back to Earth, we were fed various *BS* stories on what exactly went on between the humans and the Ursines. Some people had told us that it was all just an unfortunate moment in human history. A moment that had cost the Ursines their lives and their planet. The humans had colonized the planet a month after we got back home. I still don't know how they did it, but it only took them a week of space travel to reach the planet and rid the Ursines' home world of the rest of their species. They also found the bomb that Philip had left on the big purple giant, which in hindsight was probably a silly thing to leave on Philip's part. But luckily for him, they were none-the-wiser as to who left it there.

And I suppose I was obliged to keep it that way. I wouldn't be letting anybody in on that little secret. The other lines we were fed included such gems as "maybe your crew is just unlucky". Yeah, sure, we're unlucky enough to be banished into space by our own people, given to a bunch of savage aliens as slaves and then watch on as Earth plays a game of chess with ballistic weapons.

Sure sounds unlucky to me.

"Fencing is an art form, Flynn. You can't go into it thinking you're an artist though. Ego will take most warriors down in a flash," Teresa said, "Like this," she added, suddenly pushing me to the floor.

She stood over me, her very long legs rising up as I stared at the point of the sword she held over me. She then began to laugh, which was just as well, because I wasn't finding it the least bit funny. I didn't like being overpowered much. So it came as no surprise to me that Teresa kicking my butt at fencing didn't exactly put me in the best of moods. But she had something working in her favor that most fencing instructors didn't possess.

And that was a rocking body. My oh my was it rocking!

"The sword is up here…not wherever you're looking at," she playfully smiled.

"I wasn't looking at anything," I said, getting up to my feet.

I removed my fencing helmet and placed the thing on the ground. The metallic sheen of the helmet melded with the dark black reflection coming off the grating beneath me. Millions of tiny holes stared back up at me. For a moment or two I was transfixed by the darkness beneath me, but Teresa's shrill voice pulled me back to reality. I suppose after everything we'd been through recently; I'd become easily spaced out. Like the deep seeded terrors I'd felt back on the Ursine planet still ran through me. They still terrorized me. And nearly a month after it all, I could still feel my heart skipping a beat in my chest every once in a while.

But I was safe now. So there was no point in wallowing in what happened. But it was hard for me. I had blood on my hands. Blood I wasn't sure would ever wash off. But life went on. And I was back to work tomorrow. Back to flying missions to alien planets for Earth. Under the radar of course.

That, at least, hadn't changed.

"You okay?" Teresa asked me.

"Yeah I'm fine. It's just these clothes. They aren't that flattering. And I'm afraid the years I've spent in the Captain's chair has caused a slight mound to appear in my midsection," I smiled.

"I'd say you look just fine Flynn. Anyhow, there's a lot to prepare. We've got our first official mission tomorrow. Time to get back in the saddle and whip our asses back into shape. So no ogling my boobs, yeah?" she said, grinning at me.

I acted a little shy, but there was no point really. We knew where we stood with each other. Since getting back from the Ursine planet, we'd formed a relationship. Not a serious relationship. But a courtship. One that involved kissing and everything! I was ever so excited about that fact. Teresa was brilliant. Smart. Sexy. And above all, she was kind. Something I hadn't encountered in a woman in a very long while.

"So, back to the ship?" I asked, touching her shoulder. She nodded.

We walked hand in hand toward the changing rooms. In this particular part of the station, they'd decided to install unisex changing rooms, so we went in there together. We were alone. It was late I guess. Everybody must have been in bed. The plan was simple. We'd get changed. Grab a quick bite to eat and then board our ship, the Alpha Ship One, which was located in the shipyard, along with many other fleets that were cooling off. So we hadn't planned on taking our time. But I guess circumstances got the better of us and we ended up spending an hour in the changing rooms.

Doing what? Well, I guess whatever two people of the opposite sex do in a steamy changing room.

***

We both walked out of the changing room with smiles on our faces. Not because we'd just had the best sex we'd ever had but because we'd done it in public, and like naughty teenagers, we found it amusing that nobody was the wiser. I wish that our joy had lasted a little longer than it had, but unfortunately, an alarm sounded off all of a sudden. A loud alarm. At first, we didn't know what it was. Maybe a fire? Probably. That's what was running through my head. But then the floor lights turned red. And they only went that color in an emergency.

Times had changed. A fire wasn't really an emergency now. Every inch of the station was fitted with heat sensors. The moment the ambient level in a room went to a certain level, extinguishers would put the fire out. It was designed to sort the problem out before it even became a problem. So fires were rare, at least ones that were left to their own devices, and became big enough to set off the alarms.

So I was worried. If it wasn't a fire, then what could it possibly be?

"God, that's loud," Teresa said as she held her hands over her ears.

We'd stopped momentarily in one of the many narrow corridors on the Sector Eight Station. Seconds earlier, it had been a ghost town. You could have heard a pin drop. But now, now was different. Red lights were shining up the walls. Alarms were shrieking in my ears. Footsteps were rushing down the corridors around us. We turned a corner and saw armed troopers beckoning people over. At first, I just stood there, staring at the men in power armor suits. They wore them with pride. They were adorned in medals, insignias and metal plates. But now was not the time to stare at the shiny dangerous men.

"Come on Flynn! Something is up, we need to get to the emergency meeting point," she said, jogging toward the power armored men in front of us. I caught up with her, but a massive metal arm sprung in front of us, stopping Teresa and me from passing.

"Credentials," the man that the bulky arm belonged to spat out. His heavy breathing suggested that he was excited about something. Scared of something even. I looked up at him, his helmet covered the majority of his face. I could see my own reflection in his eyes. They stared at me as I stood there terrified, not quite sure what to say or do.

"Credentials. I need to see your credentials!" he snapped.

I looked at Teresa and then at him. My neck was hurting as I tried to keep my eyes level with his. But he was so tall and menacing that my neck was having a hard time keeping up.

"We don't have our credentials. We left them in our barracks. I didn't think we'd need them. We've been fencing and I thought…"

The man interrupted me.

"I can't let you pass unless you show me some damn I.D. Earth is being attacked. Sector Eight is on lockdown until we know who is who, and you can't come through until we know who YOU are," the guy said.

He then held his hand to his head and pressed two fingers into what I assumed was his ear. I couldn't really tell, on account of his helmet. He appeared to be listening to something. A transmission of some sort.

"What do you mean Earth is being attacked?" I asked, the reality of what was going on finally sinking in.

The man didn't reply. He just stood there and listened. I turned to Teresa, who was wide-eyed with fear. I was just about to say something when she started to scream. My attention diverted back to the power armor wearing man in front of me. He was holding his gun at me. A long thick barrel stared directly into my soul as the blackness of the muzzle seemed to be getting bigger and bigger as he stepped closer toward me.

"I'm afraid if you can't prove who you are, then I'll be forced to shoot you. Earth's orders," the Marine gruffed.

I raised my hands in the air. So did Teresa. I was just about to tell him who we were, in the hope that we'd convince him we were friendlies when the lights went off. Darkness was followed by the sound of an explosion.

And then gunfire.

Chapter Two

"We have them right where we want them. Look at all of the tiny ants scurrying below," Commander Korr's right-hand man said as he reported his findings.

The man was small in stature, yet grand in vocal delivery. He had a way about him. A villainous way. Like he was out of some sort of old-world spy movie. But the right-hand man to the feared Commander was not an old world spy. He didn't hold any old world values. He didn't follow any creeds. Nor was he one of those types that looked back at human history and yearned to experience the retro lifestyles of the citizens of Earth before they all became advanced.

No, X-O Zutor was a man of impeccable thinking. Progressive thinking. He knew where the human race was supposed to be. And equally, he was disappointed to see where they currently were. Still fighting with each other. Still spilling blood for the sake of war. But this time, things were different. Korr and the people on this ship, including the X-O, were fighting the good fight. A fight that they had to fight. If they didn't, and they let the humans of Earth carry on unscathed, then it would most likely end up badly for the whole of humanity.

And the people on this ship were not prepared to suffer for the sins of Earth. They hadn't sanctioned the baiting and extinction of the Ursine race. They had no say in it. But they recognized that it was wrong. And that's why they were attacking Earth. That's why they were doing so in the biggest non-Pilgrim-Tech-owned human fleet in space.

"Scurry away, cretins," Commander Korr said as he stood at the ship's helm, observing from the bridge. His very own worker ants were scurrying too. But not in cowardice, but in vengeance. They were scurrying toward victory. And Korr was certain that they would affirm it soon.

They just had to. There was no other possible outcome. They were just too big of a threat. They carried far too much weight. And all of that weight was crashing down on the unsuspecting people of Earth. It made Korr very happy indeed. They hadn't seen it coming. Why would they have? A giant warship approaching Earth would usually be met with some sort of radio communication. Or if deemed hostile, it would be met with brute force. But Earth didn't see them for the threat they were. All they'd seen was a human ship approaching the big blue planet. And human ships of that size were usually part of a fleet.

Fleets carried special privileges. They weren't privately owned. Well, nine times out of ten they weren't. And unfortunately for Earth, this was unlucky number ten.

"We have an incoming attempt at a video link from Earth," X-O Zutor said as he typed something into his tablet and swiped the screen. An image popped up on the ships rather large tron. **"Connecting"** appeared in the middle of the screen, and after a few seconds a face was staring back at the entire crew of the Annex Rebel Fleet.

"This is Admiral Thisk of Earth, what is the meaning of this unprovoked attack? I hope you are aware that you are attacking a sovereign planet. A planet protected by Galactic Law. This will be the end of you if you proceed any further!" Thisk said, his face going a shade of red on the video link. The quality of the video call was bad. Every now and then there was a stutter of lag, causing the high-resolution screen to tear and scramble.

"Enable face to face," Korr said, realizing that the Admiral wasn't able to see who he was talking to, or what, to be more precise, he was talking to. All the Admiral knew was that Earth was being attacked. And that quite frankly was enough for him to attempt to talk to the perpetrators, whoever they may end up being. But the Admiral wasn't expecting to see a fellow human stare back at him when the face to face camera was turned on. He knew that Earth was being attacked by a human ship, but he'd refused to believe that his own people would be responsible for such a thing.

He was of course, greatly mistaken.

"Why are you attacking us? This is an act of treason! You are one of us! You are human!" the Admiral squealed as he stared daggers at the screen.

On his end he could see the entire bridge and all the people that stood on it. There was no doubt about it. Earth was definitely not being attacked by aliens. They were being attacked by their very own kind.

"Admiral, my name is Commander Korr. The people on this ship are under my command. A command that I take quite seriously, so be assured that this isn't some kind of mistake. This isn't a blunder, fluke or misunderstanding. This is retribution. This is preservation," Commander Korr said, to a round of cheering from his cabin crew.

They were all yelling and screaming at the top of their lungs, momentarily drowning out the sound of Admiral Thisk's voice on the video chat. Korr had to gesture to his crew to be silent. They obeyed him almost immediately.

"Preservation? Of what? All you are accomplishing with this is your very own demise, Commander Korr. We are well equipped. We are battle hardened. And we certainly aren't no pushovers. So what exactly you'll accomplish out of this, other than death, is anyone's guess," Thisk said, his face growing redder by the second.

He was steaming mad. What right did these people, *ACTUAL PEOPLE*, have to attack their own planet?

Korr started to laugh as he walked closer toward the screen. Every step he took echoed in the collective silence on the bridge. His crew waited with bated breath. Korr's footsteps clunked on the metal below him. He reached the screen and put his hand on the glossy glass surface. A smile crept across his scarred face. All the while, Admiral Thisk watched on in horror, not quite understanding what was going on. All he could see was Korr's rather large hand on his own screen. He appeared to be stroking it. Gently brushing his fingers on the camera. It disturbed Thisk. He'd never seen anything like this. It was as if the man that was attacking his planet was in some sort of trance. But then the hand disappeared and Korr's scarred face glared back at Thisk. A grin, accompanied by yellow stained teeth adorned the Commander's pot-holed face.

"It's nice *to feel*, sometimes, isn't it Admiral?" Korr asked suddenly. His crew murmured in excitement. The admiral didn't say anything. He just sat there in stunned silence.

"Feeling is something us humans do on a daily basis. We feel anger. We feel pain. We feel disappointment. Those feelings are present in most people's lives. They're probably present in yours. But one thing that isn't present, is gratitude. Gratitude in being part of a species that can do as they please. And by God, you should be grateful. For if it was the other way round, and an alien race had goaded you and your people into a war that they were sure to lose, then there would be hell to pay. So think of us as an equalizer. An equalizer to a forgone conclusion. And that conclusion is the end of the human race. Because you can't keep doing what you like. You can't keep fighting the bad fight and expect to not get touched. Fear is a feeling. And I'm pretty sure you are fearful Admiral. After all, a huge warship is about to wage all-out carnage on your tiny planet. A warship that is Commanded by me. By my crew. And together, we make up your worst nightmares."

Thisk wiped the sweat off his brow and frowned.

"So you intend to make us extinct? Is that what you're saying?" he asked.

The Commander nodded his head and stepped back a few paces from the screen. He turned to his crew and raised both his arms in the air.

"You see that lads? Some intelligence. He get's it. But how much he gets, I'm not sure. But he will understand the true meaning of fear when all's said and done," Korr said, turning back around to face the screen.

"You're wrong. I don't get it," Thisk said. But then he broke into a smile of his own. "But the moment you started your attack, I sent the entire planet's Snake Pit Fighters to your bearing. By the time I finish this sentence, you'll be done."

Korr paused for effect, and raised his left hand toward the screen. He started to wag his finger at Thisk while tutting.

"You play a weak game of chess, Admiral. I am not stupid. I know of the defenses you have at your disposal. But you fail to play a good game of chess. You send your pawns. And you send plenty. For the game has just begun. And we're in this for the checkmate."

***

The gun fights are deafening as both Teresa and I duck for cover behind a partially shot through wall. The lights are out and all I can see is the occasional muzzle flash coming off somebody's Laser Omiter 9 Cannon. I didn't know what the hell was going on here. All I knew was that Earth was being attacked. And seeing how close we were to Earth, it didn't take me long to figure out that whoever was attempting to destroy the planet, was also boarding the starport and trying to wipe us out.

I wasn't really interested in the why's of the matter. To be honest, I didn't really give a hoot. All I wanted to know was where the hell could I get a gun, and protect myself from whatever this was. My question was answered almost immediately when the partially standing wall we were leaning against exploded and flung both Teresa and I onto the floor a few feet away from where we had been originally standing.

I tried to catch my breath as I lay there on the hard metal floor, staring up at what looked like a black hole, but in actual fact it was just the dense darkness that surrounded us. It was no use though. My lungs were shot to crap. I was inhaling clouds of dust from the debris that were flying around the area we were in. I say area, because I didn't know where the heck I was. I mean, we could have been anywhere on Sector Eight, but without any lighting, there was no way to know. So we were stuck. Stuck listening to whoever, or whatever was shooting their firearm in our immediate radius.

I tried to feel around for Teresa, hoping that she had landed next to me, but my hand found itself gripping some sort of cold, hard steel. I felt around a little bit more and sat up quickly when I realized that what I was touching was in actual fact a Long Barrel Laser Cannon. I hadn't seen one of those things in years. They were pretty much primitive compared to the technology that we had these days. Which made me wonder who it belonged to. I stood up, bent down, grabbed the laser cannon and cocked it. I knew how to use it because on my off days, I was known to go Laser Tag when I could. An activity I wasn't exactly proud of, but they used similar laser cannons.

Obviously not set to deadly, of course. But I doubted that the particular laser cannon in my hand was set to tickle mode. So I felt confident with it. The only problem was that I couldn't see a damn thing around me. And to make things even worse, the gunfire in the distance had stopped. Which either meant that we'd won, or I was the last man standing.

"Anyone there?" I said under my breath, which was probably the stupidest thing I could have done.

"Flynn?" I heard Teresa groan. She sounded close by. I turned around as fast as I could and beckoned her again.

"Flynn?" she groaned once more.

It sounded like she was in front of me. Maybe a hundred feet. But as I said, there was the slight problem of it being completely dark. The emergency lights had long gone out. Probably when the explosion happened. The explosion that made me and Teresa go on an unplanned flight across the vast room we were in. I assumed we were still in that room. The room just outside the changing rooms. But I was so disorientated that truth be told, we could have been dead and I wouldn't have noticed, I was that out of it.

"Flynn, I'm over…"

Silence. Just my breathing. Then nothing. Teresa stopped talking mid-sentence. But why? Was she dead. Had I just heard her die in front of me?

"TERESA!" I screamed.

But there was still no answer. Just even more silence. I stood there, laser cannon in hand, gripping the rounded cylinder shape tightly, squeezing with both my hands. I was just about to cock it when I realized I'd already done so. That, and the safety was on. I tilted my eyes toward the cannon in my hands and tried to search for the safety switch.

But then I felt a change of temperature around me. Like one minute it was ice cold. And the next it was strikingly hot. I dropped to my knees in pain, grabbed at the back of my head. I felt blood pouring out of a wound. I'd been shot! I'd been bloody shot! I frantically tried to get to my feet, but I couldn't. Something had a hold of me. My hands batted at the darkness. They felt for whoever, or whatever was holding me.

But nobody was there. It was all in my head. But I still couldn't move. It was like I'd been poisoned. And then I felt the barb. A small dart was lodged in my head. It was still stuck in there and was what was responsible for my head wound. I ripped it out and screamed. The wound itself wasn't fatal. But whatever I'd been shot with was making me woozy. I didn't understand what was going on. But I had to fight. I just had to. There was no way that I was going to allow myself to be bested again. Not after the month I'd just had.

So I got up, even if it was slowly, and sluggishly. Fortunately, once I was on my feet, I felt a little better. I flicked the switch on my cannon and turned around. I shot a blast up into the ceiling, hoping to momentarily illuminate my surroundings. And sure enough it did. For three seconds. Long enough for me to see what I was dealing with.

"What the heck?" I said groggily.

Standing meters away from me was a female holding some sort of blow pipe in her hands. She was tall, dressed in leather and wore a long trench coat. She had fingerless gloves on and what appeared to be a cape. Her hair was red and spikey and her neck had what looked like a dog collar on it. One of those ones with triangular plastic spikes protruding outwards.

"Aww, he's awake. The last one standing. And there I was thinking that I'd have a little fun with you first. But it looks like the fun is about to end ... for you at least," the weirdly dressed woman said.

I stood there shaking. I didn't know what to do. She was human. She was one of us. Not that there was any of us left standing apart from me. I just didn't understand what was going on.

"I can't shoot you. It's a Galactic crime to kill one of your own," I said, blinking hard. But it was no use. The light from the laser blast had long gone and only darkness was left.

"Don't worry honey. You don't need to do any killing around here. Just leave that to me," the woman said.

Suddenly, the hot flashing pain returned. This time it was not in the back of my head. But my chest. It forced me to drop the laser cannon. It clanged on the floor. I nearly joined the weapon for a nap, but my will to live and fight stopped me from collapsing. I put both hands on my chest and found the dart. I quickly pulled it out, but not quick enough. Before I even heard the scurry of running footsteps coming toward me, I'd been tackled to the floor. She was now on top of me. Her hands were firmly locked around my neck. She was squeezing tightly. The combination of whatever I'd been shot with and my breathing being restricted was making me fade out fast.

Permeant darkness was seeping in. But not for long. I heard a thunk. Her grip loosened on me. And then she let go. My eyes opened wide as I tried to get as much air into my lungs as I could. My breathing was raspy and my heart was pounding in my chest. My rib cage was tightening. I sat up, and winced. I started to cough, but I didn't have enough time to worry about how my health was doing. I was searching for the leather-bound girl. I needed to find her and find her fast. She was far too dangerous for me to take lightly. But instead of finding the girl, I found Teresa. It wasn't exactly hard. She was standing over me, holding her hand out. I looked up, a little disorientated.

"Is that you?" I said, my speech slurred, like I was drunk out of my mind. But I wasn't. I'd been drugged though, so not too far off. Plus it was dark, so my eyes weren't helping me out much.

"Yeah, it's me you soppy so and so. Get up. We don't have time to frolic around. The star port is being attacked."

I started to laugh.

"I'm done for the day. I've had enough frolicking around," I said, standing up. "Where's the girl," I asked.

Suddenly, I tripped and fell on my face. I scrambled back up to my feet, grabbing the laser cannon and aiming it at the floor.

"Looks like you found her!" Teresa said, pointing to a lifeless body on the hard metal floor. I cautiously prodded the motionless corpse with the barrel of the laser cannon. She didn't move. She didn't flinch. I then saw the blood pooling around the corpse and noticed the rather large combat knife stuck in the back of her head.

"Holy heck! Did you do that?" I asked, half frightened, half surprised.

"Yeah. She was all over you. Couldn't let the competition live," Teresa said. The way she was casually joking about this was making me a little wary.

"Well, I'll have you know she was only all over me because she was trying to kill me. Bitch had her hands wrapped around my neck! Not to mention that she shot me with poisonous darts – twice! I need to get myself checked out."

Teresa started to laugh.

"I know, I'm not stupid!" She said, patting me on the shoulder. "You'll have to wait till we get back to the ship to get yourself checked out. I don't know if you've noticed, but we seem to be stuck in the middle of an invasion!"

I coughed.

"Invasion! What are you on about?"

Teresa tutted and gently pushed me.

"Get a move on. We need to scram. There must be more of them."

I started to move and so did Teresa. We made our way to a doorway. I still couldn't see at all that well, but luckily my vision was getting used to the pitch-blackness that surrounded me.

"Where's everybody?" I asked.

"Dead. Looks like they're at a stalemate. But believe me, the stalemate won't last long. Before you know it, this starport will be teeming with the bastards. We need to get to the shipyard, and vacate before it's too late," Teresa said.

She began to jog down the hallway in front of us. The hallway was brighter. Light was coming from the huge bay windows on each side. Windows that were usually reserved for star gazing and admiring Earth. But when I craned my neck to the right sided window as I kept pace with Teresa, I noticed that Earth was barely visible thanks to the dense sea of warships surrounding the planet. A full-scale war was about to erupt. And we were directly in the eye of what surely was to become a massive storm.

A storm of nuclear ability, coupled with weapons capable of splitting planets in half. This wasn't going to end well.

"Let's hope we can make it off the port, or we'll have a front-row seat to the end of the world," I said, struggling for breath as we both made our way to the shipyard in search of the Alpha Ship One – in search of a safe way out of this mess.

***

EARTH. MARINE DEPLOYMENT CENTER. NEVADA. OLD USA. 18.27 HOURS.

Marine Sargent Keller stood in front of his squadron of fighters. They had been informed of the predicament that Earth now found itself in. And none of them were happy about it. They had all dreamed of the day an invasion would happen. Like in the movies of old. Ugly aliens coming to their planet in huge battlecruisers. But this was nothing like the movies. In fact, it was the opposite. That's what was making the Marines angry. If they knew how the first official invasion of Earth would go, they'd have gotten a better night's sleep the evening before.

"Okay gentlemen, it seems like we have a little problem. I've just received word that Earth and its immediate surrounding area, including the spaceports above our planet, are being attacked by a homegrown militia. Apparently, they are calling themselves the Annex Rebel Fleet. Records show that the Annex Rebel Fleet are a contingent that originally splintered off from the Letoral fleet, and as most of you know, the Letoral Fleet were best known for being homegrown terrorists. These former terrorists decided to put down their arms a long time ago, and since then, we haven't heard a peep out of them. But times have changed my friends, and these people are back, and no matter what they call themselves, they are still terrorists," Marine Sgt. Keller said, eyeing his men up as he stood in front of them.

His men stood in a line, staring back at him, eyes wide with intrigue as the information that they were receiving slowly seeped into their heads. It had been a chaotic night, the night before. Most of the Marines that stood in front of Keller were supposed to be on leave. Their six months were up, and last night they had been enjoying a much-needed break. And unfortunately for Keller and the old USA Marine Corps, the first night of leave usually involved heavy drinking.

Looking at the men in front of him, Marine Sgt. Keller could plainly see that they had taken advantage of that first night of leave. Red eyes looked back at him - bloodshot and dry - the direct result of copious amounts of alcohol and very little sleep. But none of them could have foreknown about today's events, so grilling them on their antics wouldn't get Keller anywhere, anytime soon. It would be a pointless exercise, and the Marine Sgt. didn't make a habit of partaking in such pointless pursuits.

"I know that a lot of you are not best pleased regarding your current situation. For most of you - you were only a few hours from seeing members of your family. But, I'm afraid the security and well-being of this planet far outweighs your paternal need to see your children and kiss your wives' goodnight. Earth is being attacked, and the only way that any of you will see your family again is if you fight and destroy Earth's imminent threat.

"There can be no substitutes. There will be no substitutes. Failure is not an option, and I suggest that the lot of you grow some bigger balls. You're going to need them. This Annex Rebel Fleet contingent isn't something that you should take lightly. These guys know how to fight. Their fathers were born terrorists and savages. They know how to use their weapons, and they know how to be very effective with them. So I expect that every single one of you will pay it forward so to speak," Marine sergeant Keller said, squinting as he scrutinized the men in front of him, standing in the middle of the airplane hangar, a hangar that stretched on for miles, from left to right, there was nothing but space, space for all the air vehicles that had been summoned to the strip, and were now being boarded by their pilots.

These men would accompany the pilots on board their vessels. And once they were on board, the vessels would become airborne, and join in on the defense of Earth and its space stations. Marine sergeant Keller was fully aware of the dangers that faced his men and their mission.

But Keller was not easily frightened. He was a man of integrity and decisive action. He was used to making decisions, hard decisions, decisions that affected various people. Keller knew that lives would be at risk – he also knew that some of those lives would be lost. But it would be a cold day in hell before he broke a sweat over the possibility of combat. Marines, or any of Earth's Armed Forces at that were always expected to fight and fight they shall. So there was no use in being scared of the unknown, because the unknown was exactly where men like Keller and his soldiers thrived.

"So saddle up gentlemen, I expect big things from you and your squads. This will be a day of firsts for many. It is the first time that our spaceports and space stations have been attacked by our own species. It is the first time that we as humans will fight against other humans using space-age equipment. For it was many years ago that humanity learned how to live with each other in relative peace, but now – now that has all changed. It seems as if we are regressing in time, back to an era that is now bygone. An era that is sullied by the spilled blood of our own brothers, fathers and uncles. An era where greed and lust for riches overtook humanities ability to feel empathy toward their very own species.

"It is an era that we as human's thought was gone – nothing but a distant memory. But it seems as if we were wrong, and humans still possess the ability to destroy each other's lives. So here we are gentlemen, gearing up to destroy another brother's life. So get used to the idea of sinking your teeth into the flesh of your enemy, for you will bite and claw. You will do everything in your capabilities to cut them down on the battlefield, and rip their hearts out of their chests.

It is time to rekindle the savageness that once thrived within each of our souls. It is time to become what we used to be. It is time to defend what has taken us millennia's to acquire."

The troops in front of sergeant Keller saluted him, and readied their weapons. The speech had worked, and they were ready to fight their newfound foes. It takes a lot of persuasion to convince the everyday man to take another man's life. But persuading killing machines to do their remit is not so difficult. And Keller knew that these men would get the job done. The only thing that Keller worried about was whether they'd have the stomach to go as far as he thought they would need to go. In the sergeant's experience on the battlefield, and reading testaments of wars past, Keller knew that whenever humans faced against each other, the vast bloodshed that results in such wars is usually too much for most men to deal with.

These men in particular were used to fighting aliens on simulation machines. They were used to peacekeeping missions on foreign planets. The only targets they had shot at were digital ones, ones found on target practice fields. Most of these men hadn't seen action, because humanity itself was living in peaceful times. There wasn't much need for firepower these days.

But obviously, things had changed. And as Keller stood in front of his men, a bead of sweat dropped down his back. He gritted his teeth and blinked a few times. And as his eyelids closed and opened, flashes of humanities progression flickered on the pink skin within the inside of his eyelid, projecting a historical recollection of all of humanities accomplishments.

But as he blinked again, another image popped into his head. This was more of a futuristic projection. A projection where Earth was scorched by war, and men were deformed from combat. The image only lasted a second, but within that second, Keller saw the mighty torrent of death that was the result of humanities inevitable implosion. An implosion that could only be brought on by the continuous infighting of its species. It was a ghastly sight. But the sergeant couldn't rely on his deepest fears to lead his men into battle successfully. It was normal for him to be apprehensive of the repercussions of such a war between two human factions. But, much worse had happened in the past, and humanity had managed to dig itself out of the depths of hell before, to rise back to the top, and become an ever-present force in the Galaxy.

Keller just hoped that they could do it all over again once this was over and done with. For he feared for planet Earth's future. A future where humanity was divided yet again. A future where all of Earth's accomplishments were foreshadowed by the dark and gloomy cloud of civil strife that engulfed the planet. A shadow that would cast its ugly darkness across every city and every dwelling on Earth, and quite possibly across the Milky Way Galaxy itself. He feared how other alien species would react to such a civil war. The only reason that humanity found itself within the coalition of Galaxies and other alien species, was because they had managed a thousand years of peace and prosperity on their very own planet. And now that peace and prosperity was dwindling fast, only the stars and Gods above them all knew of their fate.

And it was a fate that sergeant Keller and his men would fight to the death for.

"Dismissed gentlemen. May the Universe be kind to you in battle. Be safe and above all, come back home in one piece," sergeant Keller said, saluting his men and watching as they started jogging off toward the tarmac, where hundreds of ships lay in wait for them.

Keller watched on as his men boarded various ships. Some of them were troop carriers, while others were full-blown warships. Ships so large that they overshadowed much of the entrance of the hangar that Keller stood in. Huge ominous shadows cascaded across the floor, scattering up toward Keller as he stood there in awe, watching the ships take off into the night sky. The sun was setting on this perilous day, and in the creeping darkness of the early night sky awaited the Annex Rebel Fleet.

Once those ships reached their targets, Keller could only hope that they would put an end to what could possibly be the actual end of Earth.

"Godspeed," Keller said as he watched the last ship exit the atmosphere and turn into a glistening dot in the sky, joining the millions of other dots laden in the sheet of black that covered the majority of the atmosphere.

Keller wondered how many of those dots were dying stars, and how many more of them were rebel ships baying for blood. Keller was hoping that his men would get the job done. He had all the faith in the world in them, but that didn't stop the pit of his stomach from churning. He had a bad feeling, a feeling that was slowly rising up his esophagus, causing the acidic remnants of his dinner to scorch the back of his throat.

In Keller's line of work, a gut feeling is to be ignored. From very early on, all the way back to basic training, men are told to ignore their feelings. It is the only way that they can become the killing machines that the State wants them to be. But Keller was one of the Old Guard, a Guard that believed in gut feelings. And his gut feeling was telling him that this could quite possibly be unwinnable for them. From what he heard from Command, there were many many ships awaiting their imminent arrival. Ships that were decked with up-to-date technology, a technology that in the right hands could destroy worlds and planets. But he did have a trump card, and that trump card was a ravenous squad of Marines that wouldn't take too kindly to opposition.

He just hoped that was enough.

Chapter Three

My heart thumped in my ears as Teresa and I ran down a corridor. It was a corridor that I didn't recognize. I'd been on Sector Eight for a month now, and I'd never run down this corridor before. Hell – I'd never even walked down it. This particular spaceport was much bigger than I originally thought. And for the majority of the month that I had spent onboard this spaceport, I'd found refuge in the bar, drinking myself stupid along with Dale Dykstra and Philip. But I hadn't seen them for a few days, and had spent most of my free time with Teresa. I was glad that she was with me, even when all of this madness had kicked off. I couldn't imagine being with anybody else, well, maybe Dale, after all, he is quite large and is super handy with his fists.

But Teresa was just as handy. And to be honest, I was astonished that she was even able to fight, let alone plunge a knife into the back of another person's head. What she did was technically murder, killing another human being is a Capital Crime, both on Earth and within the Galactic Law boundaries of allies that surround us. But it seems like things have changed. Within seconds, my instincts were telling me that killing humans would no longer be frowned upon. And it seemed as if we had some new friends to thank for that.

And those friends were currently fighting in dogfights with our very own army. An army that was originally sanctioned to defend Earth from any possible alien threats. But if the woman Teresa had knifed was connected somehow to the attack on this spaceport, then it seemed as if we had a new mission directive. And the army that was once sanctioned to protect us from aliens would now be sanctioned to kill other human beings.

That's why the Marines in power armor earlier had not wanted to let us pass. They knew what was going on, and were well aware of the fact that we were being attacked by a splinter group of people.

People once loyal to the regime. People once loyal to Earth. So it made sense that they had wanted to see my I.D. Unfortunately, the lights had gone out, and the spaceport had been invaded. Granted, the woman in leather had been the only enemy I'd seen so far, but I couldn't ignore the nagging feeling in the pit of my stomach, the feeling telling me that the game had changed, and Earth was no longer united. I hadn't had time to assume anything other than that. But if I had had the time to think things through a little more precisely, I might have connected the Alpha Ship One and our previous mission to this possible crack in Earth's current peace among its people.

But running down the corridor was dividing my attention. I didn't have enough time to think. For all I knew, this was something else entirely. And if I hadn't seen the woman in leather, I wouldn't be none the wiser to the current political climate we found ourselves in. I also wouldn't have put two and two together, and assumed that humanity was falling apart in front of my own two eyes.

Everything that Earth and Pilgrim Tech had ever worked for was corroding. The virus was multiplying. The lies were bubbling to the surface. And before I knew it, everybody would know. Everybody would know what Earth, Pilgrim Tech and the Alpha Ship One had done to the Ursines. And if the corridor we were running down wasn't dividing my attention, I would have probably been in a major panic right about now. I would probably be trying to think of a faster, more dangerous way to get myself off the spaceport and onto the Alpha Ship One. And once I was on that ship, I'd probably hit the boosters and get out of dodge, never to return and leave the humans to settle their differences while I sipped on cocktails and kissed my girl.

For if I knew what was in my future, I'd definitely be doing that. But, you know what they say about hindsight, 20/20 vision and all. Now I can kick myself for not thinking straight, but back then, back on that spaceport, back running down that corridor, all I knew to be true was that Teresa and I were in immediate danger. And the origins of that danger was not important. All that was important was that Teresa and I manage to get to safety. That's where my priorities were. But as I said, if only I knew.

"What the hell is going on?" Teresa said, running beside me, bay windows to our left and right, lights flashing as various spaceships shot at each other, some exploding, some escaping death.

It was such chaos, I found it hard to focus. The corridor was bright on account of the vigorous fighting on the outside. Fighting that was far too close for comfort. But we had to carry on. We had to get off the ship. No matter what was going on outside, mine and her safety was paramount.

"I don't know, but I have a bad feeling about this. Those ships look human. They look like our own ships. Not to mention the lady in leather, the one that you saved me from. She was trying to kill me. Where the hell did she come from? Are there more of them? And what the hell do they want? I thought we were the same! Humans don't fight humans!" I said, nearly tripping on a loose wire on the floor, but jumping to avoid it.

The corridor was ending, and there was a hard right. Both Teresa and I took that hard right, our legs aching as we continued to run. We entered another room. This room was larger than the other one - the one outside of the changing areas. It was dark, some of the lighting above us was flickering and flailing as it tried to illuminate the spacious room, but the power onboard Sector Eight was dwindling, and I had a feeling that the firefight between the various ships orbiting the spaceport had something to do with it.

The longer the dogfights outside lasted, the more likely a stray laser beam shot or missile could hit the spaceport. And a single hit from any of those ships could destroy the exterior of the space station. A single hole caused by such a hit could rip and shred Sector Eight, sucking me and Teresa out into the vacuum of space, suffocating us and causing our demise. So getting to the Alpha Ship One was our priority. But the thing is, I'd never taken this route before, and was confused.

"I have no idea where we are, or how the hell we are getting to the ship. I'm counting on you here Teresa," I said, momentarily stopping to catch my breath. Teresa did the same, sweat dripping down her face as she looked left and right, surveying the strange room in front of us.

I say strange because neither of us seemed to know where the hell we were. But besides from that, the room was pretty much identical to the many other areas and rooms onboard Sector Eight. Earth had a habit of employing simple architecture when it came to official government space stations. Each room was bland and equally depressing. In my travels, I'd been on board many different spaceports'. Some of them in far away Galaxies. And I'd have to say that Earth's spaceports were the most confusing of the lot. They were like mazes. And I felt like a rat. A rat being experimented on. But unfortunately, this wasn't controlled. There wasn't a scientist in a lab coat waiting to tell me that I had passed the test.

This was all real. And there was no escaping that fact.

"I think I know where we are. A few days ago I was wondering the corridors, looking for something to do. You know how it is Flynn; life can get boring onboard, so I thought I'd have a wander. In my extracurricular excursion, I think I came across this room. If I'm not mistaken, the shipyard is just through here," Teresa said, holding my hand, trying to reassure me with a smile.

But it would take more than a smile to make me feel at ease. I was still panting for breath when the flickering lights above us popped and hissed suddenly, like they'd all blown their fuse. Glass and plastic shards came falling from above, landing on me and Teresa.

And then there was an explosion. An explosion that rattled the walls around us. At first, I thought that maybe one of the ships outside had inadvertently hit the spaceport. But then I heard footsteps. They were close by. In this room in fact. The footsteps were loud and ominous.

And from the collective crescendo of light taps on the metal floor, I surmised that the footsteps belonged to a group of people. People wearing armor. The sounds of their guns being held tightly in their hands squeaked in my ears. The hushed whispers between those armed people were barely audible to me, but I could pick up the fact that they were indeed talking. I couldn't hear what they were saying, but I could tell that they were a mere ten to twenty feet from us. I shoved Teresa to the ground and joined her on the floor, putting my fingers to my lips, signaling her to stay silent.

The footsteps continued, the sound of boots clunking on the floor as they walked through the room. They didn't stop - they didn't see us - but I knew that they weren't friendly. I could tell by the atmosphere in the room. It was as if the thermostat had been turned to zero, and a cold chill rattled down my spine.

They continued to walk and talk quietly, conspiring in hushed voices, the sound of metal flexing and plastic cracking under their boots. After twenty to thirty more seconds of uncertain silence, I came to the conclusion that they had passed us by, probably walking into another room, in search of their next victim. I dreaded to think of the carnage and destruction that these individuals had already caused.

The very fact that they were on board Sector Eight meant that they were a force to be reckoned with. I didn't hold any hopes of rescue, and I knew that the Marines that usually patrolled these hallways and corridors and rooms were now most likely dead. So that only meant one thing; if we stayed where we were, cowering in the darkness, we'd also end up dead. It was most definitely time to get off Sector Eight.

"We should go before they come back," I said, holding on to the laser cannon that I had scavenged off the girl in leather.

Teresa still had the knife, the same knife that she had stuck into that girl in leather, but even I knew that a knife and a plasma gun was no match against a squadron of armed men.

"I agree, from what I remember, the shipyard is on the left," Teresa said, whispering as she slowly stood up. I also got up, holding onto the laser cannon, tightly gripping it as I tried to squint, attempting to get a better look at my surroundings.

"I think they went right," I said, holding the canon tightly, aiming it as I squinted.

"Well, it's just as well they went right, because we are going left," Teresa said, slowly walking off and doing just that.

Me and Teresa hugged the wall as we crouched our way through the darkness. Plastic and glass shards cracked under our boots, but we remained steadfast and continued through the darkness. After a minute or so, we reached a pile of rubble, rubble that once belonged to a door. A door that hung on the left. And once we walked through it, we'd be on our way toward the shipyard. I turned toward Teresa and tried to summon a smile. And even though she couldn't see my face, and I could barely see hers, I knew from her warm touch as she grabbed my hand that no matter what happened next; we'd have each other's back.

"Follow my lead," I said, carefully stepping over the rubble and walking into the unknown. Teresa followed closely behind.

***

"Target coming up on my left," the lead Snake Pit Fighter said as he locked his hand firmly around the controls, his head swooning from left to right as he surveyed the battlefield in front of him.

He was joined by nine other Snake Pit Fighters. They were trailing behind him, keeping close to his back, each ship inches away from the other, flying in a formation that they had practiced before. Their training was all that these pilots had when it came to fighting other airborne enemies. Most of their time had been spent in the simulation computer. They had run drills on various scenarios, going over every possible situation on the battlefield.

The lead Snake Pit Fighter was nervous. The last time he was in a simulator, he'd racked up seven fails. The last fail was the worst one of them all. He'd managed to crash the ship that he was flying into a canyon. There were no canyons here, so at least he had that going for him.

The other Snake Pit Fighters were doing the same, locking their hands on their controls, fiddling with switches and checking their ships vitals. It was all standard procedure before coming face-to-face with enemy contact. And they were seconds away from that contact. In front of them, careening within the darkness of space, hovering above the starport, were hundreds of enemy ships. Some of them were big, while others were small. But all of them were dangerous. And all of them were heading their way. If the Snake Pit Fighters didn't act soon, then they would be swarmed by the enemy ships. So quick thinking was a must.

"Multiple enemies in my sights," the lead snake fighter said, locking on to one of the nearest enemy ships, and pushing down on the fire button.

Suddenly, a swarm of red-nosed missiles left the comfort of his ships Ironsides and dazzled their way toward the enemy target. Within the blink of an eye, the missiles hit their target, reducing one of the ships into nothing but rubble floating in the vacuum of space, shards of metal cascading off the horizon - the other ships that surrounded it were ducking and diving for cover.

"Target destroyed, I repeat target destroyed," the lead Snake Pit Fighter said, his hand still hovering above the controls, gripping at the joysticks, sweat falling down the nape of his neck.

His helmet was itchy, the hair on his head sticking against the glass and plastic covering his skull. All he wanted to do was scratch his head, but he had a lot of work to do. And when there was work to do, there was no room for error. Especially on the battlefield.

While it was true that he did have backup, he knew that the enemy far outnumbered him and his men. So evasive maneuvers would be necessary. And every single Snake Pit Fighter would have to be on their game.

"Okay gentlemen, let's show these guys how it's done," the lead Snake Pit Fighter said. With another enemy in his sights, he pressed the fire button, and watched as more missiles flew toward yet another unsuspecting target.

Another confirmed hit and another enemy down.

But now, now they had bigger problems. The Snake Pit Fighters didn't have the element of surprise anymore. The enemy had seen them coming, and now they were retaliating in force. So the game plan had changed, and all ten of them would have to be thinking out of the box if they were to get out of this one alive.

"On my mark, I want all of you to split up. We need to be hitting them like a swarm of bees, and the only way we're going to manage to take them down is if the swarm splits and hits them from every possible angle," the lead Snake Pit Fighter said, summoning some inner strength and guts, breathing through his nose and counting down to ten in his head.

Everything was working out just how he'd planned. The enemy were reacting in a predictable manner. If they continued doing so, it would cost them their fleet. The Snake Pit Fighters were well trained and well-equipped. But unpredictability was their weakness. And even though the enemy ships were acting predictable at the moment, nothing was guaranteed in the heat of battle. So the lead Snake Pit Fighter knew that if they were to win this particular battle, and defend the starport from total destruction, they'd need to dispatch of the enemy fighters in record time.

"Three... Two... One... Split!" The lead Snake Pit Fighter said, pulling the controls back, his fighter ship climbing, the nose of the ship pointing at a ninety-degree angle. The other Snake Pit Fighters did the same. They swarmed around the enemy ships, striking from every possible angle.

But the enemy were prepared. And they had defenses of their own. The Snake Pit Fighters didn't know it yet, but their ordeal had only just begun.

***

I couldn't quite believe it but we had just reached the shipyard. Teresa and I were panting for breath as we entered the large and ominous yard, which looked haunted and derelict in its current state. The shipyard was usually bustling with activity, hundreds of ships being worked on, hundreds of workers talking with fellow pilots, stocking the ships with supplies before they had to leave.

But right now, things were different. There were hardly any ships in the yard, and there were no workers. There had been workers, but unfortunately they were no longer with us anymore. Strewn on the floor, every couple of yards, were dead bodies. The dead bodies belonged to the former shipyard employees. Most of them were male. All of them were still wearing their high visibility jackets. Next to them, were a couple of Marines.

It seemed as if the Marines had attempted to thwart the onslaught from the invading enemy presence on board the star port. But it hadn't worked out in their favor. They had lost. Now, the starport was teeming with savage soldiers, soldiers trying to dismantle both the port and the people on board it. I guess seconds earlier, when Teresa and I found ourselves hiding in the darkness from the footsteps, footsteps belonging to those savage soldiers, they'd just returned from their heinous acts. Hundreds of bodies lay on the floor, riddled with bullets, shot like dogs and left to die.

There wasn't anything that Teresa and I could have done. They were long gone – as were the soldiers that had executed them, yet we were still in danger. Hanging around and mourning the loss of these men and women wasn't going to bring them back. In fact, if we hung around long enough, all we'd end up doing is being taken out - like our friends on the floor - bullet holes in our heads and our torsos – and that wouldn't accomplish much.

So, me and Teresa didn't hang around, we carefully stepped over the dead bodies and made our way toward the Alpha Ship One, which was the only ship left in the yard. It seemed as if all the other ships had bailed on the starport. As soon as trouble had made itself known, the various captains on board had decided to get out as soon as they could. And I would have done the same thing if only I hadn't been on the opposite side of the port.

Strategically speaking, this particular station wasn't easy to traverse during an emergency. And as I said before, it was more akin to a maze than a functioning starport. If it had been up to me, after this was all over - *if* we all survived that is - the first thing I'd be doing is contacting the Galactic Empire, and maybe suggesting to them that they needed to rethink their architectural design of their ports. After all, the people on the floor, the dead ones all around me that is, would probably agree with my presumptive suggestions. Because if it wasn't for the mightily confusing layout of this port, then maybe it wouldn't be so damn easy to infiltrate it or so hard to escape it.

Just a thought…

"There it is!" Teresa said, hopping over a few more dead corpses, trying not to give them much attention.

She was a fragile girl as it was, and even though she had already shown some hardness in her personality, especially when she'd managed to defend me from the girl in leather earlier, she still held an admirable quality of empathy about her.

I could tell that she was upset over the carnage that these invaders had caused on our temporary home. I could also tell that she had vengeance in her eyes, and when she'd spotted the Alpha Ship One hovering in the distance, I could see that she wanted nothing more than to board the ship, take off, and blast the people responsible into oblivion.

"Come on, let's get out of here," I said, grabbing Teresa's hand and guiding her toward the ramp that led up toward the Alpha Ship One.

Most of what had happened so far had been nothing but a blur. Whilst in perilous danger, the human body has a habit of heightening the senses. And with that habit comes the undesirable effect of memory loss. The body is so overloaded with emotion and heightened sense, that the brain cannot keep up with the arduous task of storing certain information. Like in the midst of a heated argument with somebody, it's always difficult to remember what was said, or how it was said. And just like that, right then at that moment in time, my mind was all over the place.

There were chunks of memory that had disappeared from my recollection. Like what was said during our walk up the slope, toward the Alpha Ship One. I know something was said, but for the life of me I cannot remember. All I can remember though is the fact that both Teresa and I were more than happy to reach our ship. And even though there were hundreds of dead bodies below, we felt a certain happiness knowing that we were seconds away from leaving this dangerous port.

"Open the door," Teresa said, giving me a frightened glance over my shoulder, checking if there was anybody behind us. I did as she said, grabbing my ship key and swiping it over the sensor. Suddenly, the double doors opened and we scrambled inside, I then swiped the key once again to lock the door behind us.

"We made it!" I said, still trying to catch my breath as I placed the key back in my pocket and raised my head up to look at Teresa.

I expected to see a smile on her face, but was met with an expression of fear. Right then I knew that something was wrong. Turning around, my worst fears came to life, beating against my insides like a barbed-wire-batt. Standing on the deck, pointing their weapons at us, were four heavily armed humans.

"Looks like we have a few stragglers," one of the armed men said, slowly making his way up toward me and Teresa.

I was dumbfounded and didn't know what to do. Part of me wanted to fight, to hit out and protect Teresa and my ship. But the other part of me was subdued and frightened. It was like there was a battle going on within the middle of my head. It was ripping and tearing at both sides of my brain. The side of my brain that said fight or flight, and the other side, the rational side, the logical side. But in a situation like this, thinking wasn't going to get me out of danger. They say that a strategic and calculated mind wins on the battlefield, but sometimes – just sometimes – straight out violence trumps everything.

"To hell with this!" I said, pulling my hand back and landing a stiff shot onto the approaching man's jaw.

He wasn't expecting it. The look on his face said it all, really. He was in shock, as was I, but within the few seconds of shock that proceeded my outburst, I managed to grab the man's sidearm, and was now aiming it squarely at his head. The others had raised their guns higher and were now approaching Teresa and I. But as soon as they saw that I had his weapon pointing directly at him, they startled and stopped where they stood.

"That's not wise," the man said, visibly shaken up, a welt forming under his eye where I'd smacked my knuckles against his face.

But before I could retort, I heard something behind the three of them. A mighty crash of some sorts. Followed by footsteps. The three men turned on their heels, and were met by some aggressive opposition. I couldn't see all that well, on account of the man I had directly in front of me blocking my vision, but I heard some screams followed by some gargles and then the collective sound of three bodies hitting the ground.

The man I had in my sights quaked in his boots slightly as he stared at me, shivering and stuttering as he realized that the tables had been turned. He immediately dropped his weapon, the sound of it clanging off the metallic floor. He now had his hands up, and moved slightly to the side as I pushed past him, still holding my weapon at him. What I saw behind the man at first frightened me, but then comforted me. Standing at attention with smiles on their faces, both Dale Dykstra and Philip saluted me as they stood over the incapacitated bodies of the three men that'd had their guns pointed at us seconds before.

"Where the hell did you two come from?" I asked, patting Dale on the shoulder. He smiled at me as if to shrug off the question. Philip came closer and gave me a hug. Dale did the same, and squeezed the two of us.

"Guys? What about him?" Teresa said, holding the other man by the scruff of his neck.

The three of us turned around and saw Teresa grabbing at the lone survivor. My heart quickened a little in my chest, knowing that we most likely would have to kill him as well. I wasn't good with that sort of thing. I preferred that other people did the dirty work when it came to death and destruction around here. But I wasn't stupid either, and I knew that we couldn't keep him as a pet. But before I could even make a decision, Dale Dykstra had walked over toward him, his heavy gigantic frame looming over the scared-stiff man and cocked back his huge fist and landed a stern shot to the bloke's head.

The man hit the deck, his head smashing against the metal beneath him. Dale stood over him, a smug look on his face, and smiled back at me.

"Might as well see what he knows," I said, smiling back at Dale, and then looking at the three bodies behind me.

Dale and Philip had disarmed the three men on the floor via violent means. It had taken me a few seconds to realize, but Philip had a bloodied knife in his hands. And Dale had blood-soaked hands. So unfortunately, the three men behind us were useless. They were very much dead, but in my mind I had already justified their deaths, even though I had nothing to do with it.

They would have killed us in a heartbeat. If it wasn't for Dale and Philip already being on board the ship without the other men knowing, then it could have been us on the floor instead.

"We need to get off this starport *ASAP*," I said, stepping over the three dead bodies on the floor and making my way toward the captain's seat. I turned the power on, the engines idling, and did a quick systems diagnostic check. Everything came back 100% operational. I nodded at the others and ushered them toward their seats.

"What about the dead bodies?" Philip asked.

I shrugged my shoulders.

"Well, I guess can jettison them once we are in orbit," I said, flicking a few switches and pressing a few buttons, starting the inaugural liftoff process.

"How about sleeping beauty over there?" Teresa asked.

I sighed, slowly pushing the power lever up, the sound of the Alpha Ship One's engines roaring to life.

"When he wakes up, we ask him what this is all about," I said, fielding off any remaining questions by getting the ship's power to a hundred percent and disengaging from the shipyard dock.

Before we knew it, we were hurtling out of one of the exit tunnels of the starport. Within a few seconds, we had entered low orbit space, just above Earth's atmosphere. A battle was still being waged around us as we attempted to leave the LEO (Low Earth Orbit) of the space station. Hundreds of ships were dogfighting amongst each other. I turned to the others and gave them a nervous frown.

"Looks like we have some ducking and diving to do," I said, maxing out the throttle and preparing myself for some evasive maneuvers.

Chapter Four

Commander Korr was overlooking the holographic schematic map in front of him. The hologram was rising from his workstation, showing the position of his men on the battlefield. From the comfort of his commanding chair he could overlook a live feed of the battlefield, seeing how his men stacked up against the enemy forces of Earth. He was pleased with how his battalion were successfully fending off the advances coming from the well-prepared humans. The Commander knew that the humans were both efficient and deadly.

Korr wasn't an idiot, and knew that if he and his men were going to overthrow Earth's fleet, then they would need to think fast and act just as swiftly. Korr had a few ideas of his own. The Commander knew that his success on the battlefield totally relied on the efficiency of his own men. It was a give and take situation. His men needed to be just as prepared as Earth's fleet. If they took their enemy for granted, then a surefire loss was most likely on the cards for them.

And war is very much a game of cards. A lot of the time, war is likened to chess. And while chess is a game of strategic traits, war has other ingredients mixed into its proverbial deck. While chess is a static game of war fought between inanimate pieces, war is fought between organic life matter. And frankly speaking; the total objective of most wars is to annihilate the organic matter that stands in the aggressor's way.

So as Commander Korr stared at his holographic schematic in front of him, he thought of the various ways that his men could succeed in the forthcoming battle that was looming ever so near. The Commander made sure that he and his men were not ill-prepared and that they had a few aces up their sleeves. And just like war was not only a game of chess, but a game of cards, the ace that the Commander had up his sleeve was the dark horse in this escapade.

He just needed to know when to use it.

In poker, it is wise to use a dark horse or wildcard straightaway. For it is a turn-based game. But unfortunately for Commander Korr and his Annex Rebel Fleet, this wasn't Civilization the video game. There were no turns, and diplomacy was not an option. There was no negotiating with these people. For they had sullied the human name, and the history that came with it. And in Commander Korr's mind, they had to pay for their sins.

He was about to make sure that they paid in full.

"Send out overwatch," Commander Korr said, standing up and addressing his men. X-O Zutor stood beside Commander Korr. He had a smile on his face, but as the Commander's words left his mouth, the smile on Zutor's face disappeared, and a nervous grimace adorned his ruddy features instead.

"But sir, do you not think it is too soon in the game to bring out overwatch?" X-O Zutor said.

The Commander shook his head.

"It is never too soon to bring out overwatch," he said.

X-O ZUTOR nodded faithfully and turned toward the others.

"You heard the Commander, send out overwatch," he said, addressing the others around him.

The big burly Commander sat back in his chair, and watched the schematic hologram on his workstation. He sat there for a few minutes, waiting for his command to come to fruition. And sure enough, after a minute or so, he saw overwatch appear on the map.

There were four dots on the screen, each one of them represented an overwatch unit. Separately, they were massive warships. They had the capability of landing planetside, and disbursing a few thousand troops onto the ground.

On board the Commander's overwatch battalion were some of his best men. And he would need all the men he could get to overthrow Earth's defenses. The Commander wasn't stupid; he knew that this excursion only served to put fear into Earth's heart. The Annex Rebel Fleet wasn't big enough to invade Earth and take on its defenses. But it was big enough to prove a point. And that point was simple; people couldn't go about doing what they pleased anymore. Earth had gotten too big for its boots, and it was about time someone took them down a peg or two.

"Sir, overwatch has been intercepted. Three of the ships have been destroyed. Only one of them remains. What's our next move?" The Commander's right-hand man said, sidling up beside him and watching the massacre on the schematic hologram on his workstation unfold.

Commander Korr had been far too distracted to keep up with the action unfolding in front of his very eyes. But when he saw that overwatch had been compromised, his heart sank and an uncontrollable anger rose up within him.

"Son of a bitch!" The Commander said, lashing out at the air and knocking over some of the clutter on his workstation.

Papers and cups flew off the workstation and landed on the floor, clattering about as the ship shook slightly. The dogfighting between the Annex Rebel Fleet and the Snake Pit Fighters was becoming overbearing. The Commander didn't know how much more of a pounding his men and his ships could take. He had to think things through a little more thoroughly.

He needed to be smart, and to save this mission, he would need to retreat. But this was far from over, and he still had his ace firmly up his sleeve. Overwatch was merely the first phase.

"Tell our men to retreat, we'll hit them where it hurts soon enough, but for now, self-preservation is our only mission. We can't play our hand too early," the Commander said, turning toward the controls and sitting back down on his seat.

X-O Zutor was picking up the papers that'd been flung off the Commander's workstation, and was placing them back in order.

"Sir, I'm picking up an unidentified ship leaving Sector Eight. And I'm afraid I have some bad news," one of the men behind him said, forcing the Commander to swivel in his chair to face the music.

"Well, don't just stand there stuttering, tell me what the news is!" The Commander said, his teeth snarling over his lips like a feral dog's prominent overbite.

"I'm picking up a trace marker onboard the unidentified ship. It seems as if they have one of our men. He still alive," the man said, still stuttering but managing to get his words out just fine in the end.

The Commander's face was a picture - a picture of red and purple - anger and disdain. An artery in his neck bulged as his face went red. In no circumstances could he let the people of Earth hold one of his men captive. They could not know the extent of the danger they were in. They could not know the Commander's plans. So a preemptive strike was in order. And the Commander didn't hesitate in delivering such an emphatic strike.

"Take the ship out. No survivors."

The Commander's sidekick looked at him with a surprised expression on his face. He held the Commander's gaze for a few seconds and then looked at the floor.

"But sir, we can't just kill one of our own," X-O Zutor said, still staring at the floor, not daring to look his Commander in the eye.

"Don't you understand? If we let them live, then we all die! Nobody can know about the Annex Fleet or its plans. And I'm afraid that we have a liability onboard that ship. I cannot trust that whoever they have on that ship won't talk. And believe me, if he does talk, that means the end for all of us!" The Commander said, a solemn and reflective silence followed his speech.

But that eerie silence was soon followed by the sound of his orders being obeyed. The weapons expert lined the ship up in his sights, his hands hovering over the engagement button. He turned toward the Commander and waited for his final order.

Commander Korr didn't say anything. All he did was nod his head, and the weapons expert engaged the target.

"Target locked – firing…"

***

The lead Snake Pit Fighter caught a glimpse of something on the right of his heads-up display. At first, he didn't know what it was. It could have been a reflection coming from one of the stars nearby. Or, as his gut was telling him, somebody was about to use what's referred to as an *endgame missile*. The Snake Pit Fighter had seen those types of missiles being used before. And his training had made him aware of the tell-tale signs of one about to go into commission. The thing with endgame missiles was; they were usually used as a last ditch result. These missiles were used in desperate times, and the way that his team had been performing, he knew that the people they were up against were possibly losing their bottle. This was the first time that he or his crew had faced other human beings before, but that didn't mean he wasn't privy to their faults and various character traits.

In all his years of fighting, he got to know men well – so well it was scary. He knew how they would usually react in tense situations and standoffs. And now was no different. He was fighting other men. Men that wanted to destroy Earth. Men that were willing to go against the system, to buck the trend, to be a grain of sand in a deep desert, a deep desert lacking an oasis of hope.

But as a Snake Pit Fighter, he also knew that fighting the establishment was futile. Men have tried in the past and failed. And now was no different, men were attempting to rise up against the tides of the vicious sea, but the sea proved too strong for them. And that is why this particular ship was about to use an endgame missile. It was textbook stuff. When the going gets tough, the tough get going – and *the tough* wanted to end this before it even started.

"Contact on my far right, endgame missile about to be used, I repeat – endgame missile about to be used, evasive maneuvers – evasive maneuvers!" The lead Snake Pit Fighter said from within his cockpit, sweat dripping down his face, the interior of his space helmet fogging up as he attempted to get a lock on the huge mothership that was about to commission the endgame missile into existence.

"Any suggestions?" Another pilot said, his voice coming through the lead Snake Pit Fighter's intercom.

"I suggest we do something about it – we can't let them win now can we?" The pilot replied, his hands on his flight sticks, veering right, the ship tilting as he tried to get a better lock-on on the mothership.

"Stick to formation, hit hard and fast, and keep on the captain's tail," another pilot said, bringing a forced smile to the lead Snake Pit Fighters face. Even though he was sweating profusely and seriously nervous about taking on such a huge ship, he knew that he couldn't allow the enemy to fire such a devastating blow upon one of his own vessels.

A thought suddenly popped into his head; which ship was the perpetrator aiming at? For him to be able to intercept the missile when it fired eventually, which wouldn't be too long, he figured he had a couple more seconds of thinking time to work things out, yet he still had to pinpoint the target.

So he scanned the immediate battlefield in front of him. His Snake Pit team lagged behind, flanking on his back, providing covering fire from other ships. In total there were eight enemy ships in front of him. Unlike in video games, the ships didn't have red triangles above them, indicating friend or foe. But he did have something working in his favor, and that was the onboard computer. It was able to pick up tracer elements on the ships in front. Elements that told him whether the ship was commissioned by Earth's Galactic Empire or whether they were unmarked vessels.

These particular vessels in front of him were all unmarked. Bar from one. A large ship.

The ship looked as if it had seen better days. From what he could see from where he was, the mysterious ship was a haulage ship. It was used in resource gathering missions. And a ship like that wasn't heavily armed. Sure, it had some forms of self-defense, a light shield and a few heavy armor piercing Gatling guns on the Ironsides, but besides from that it was a sitting duck.

The onboard computer was telling the lead Snake Pit Fighter that this ship was called the Alpha Ship One. A clearance level appeared on his LCD screen on his heads-up-display within the interior of his helmet. The clearance level stated that the Alpha Ship One was a high priority vessel. That meant that it was a high-value target for the enemy. And the fact that it was trying to flee the Sector Eight starport meant that the enemy had it in their sights.

So now that the lead Snake Pit Fighter could see what the mothership was targeting, he was able to judge the trajectory of the potential missile shot. As he sat there in his pilot's seat, sweat still dripping down his face, he tried to steady his ship a little. The other Snake Pit Fighters behind him were fielding off various shots from the mothership's accompanying fleet. But as the seconds ticked by, he noticed that most of the ships were beginning to retreat. The only ship that was showing any form of aggression was the mothership.

And he knew exactly where that aggression would end at.

"What's going on? Why hasn't it fired yet?" One of the pilots asked, his voice sounding echoey in the lead Snake Pit Fighter's ear.

"He's charging up the beam. It looks as if our friends are adding a little more spunk to this missile, so the rest of you should hold back, this is gonna be quite a blast," the lead Snake Pit Fighter said, angling his ship toward the mothership which hung in the void of space, just above planet Earth, tilting slightly as it tried to align itself with the Alpha Ship One which was still attempting to hurtle away from the battlefield.

"Here she blows!" One of the pilots said, the one nearest to the lead Snake Pit Fighter.

They were now in an arrow formation, pointing at the mothership, waiting for her to make her move, much like in a game of chess, but they knew their place, they were the pawns, and she was most definitely the Queen.

Suddenly, the mothership fired its payload toward the Alpha Ship One which was ducking and diving between the other warships. The missile arced in the void slightly, the stars around it twinkling off the luminous glare emanating from the metallic surface of the missile. It seemed as if the rocket hovered slightly for a few seconds, as if it couldn't make its mind up on how to approach the Alpha Ship One.

But finally, after two seconds, it got a hard lock on the spaceship, and pinged itself toward the vessel.

The Alpha Ship One dodged and weaved through the remainder of the enemy warships, and nearly crashed against a satellite dish attached to the star port. But fortunately, they managed to get past the starport and were now near open space where the missile was seconds away from hitting the back of the large ship. But the lead Snake Pit Fighter had the missile in his sights and locked on to the deadly artillery, firing at it, holding his breath until impact.

"Holy heck, what a shot!" Somebody yelled through the intercom, followed by cheering and hollering.

The lead Snake Pit Fighter smiled as he watched the missile erupt into a ball of flames, narrowly missing the fleeing Alpha Ship One. He disabled his lock on and disengaged his weapons. Breathing heavily, fogging up the interior of his visor, he sighed in relief.

"I'm getting far too old for all this malarkey," was all the pilot could say as he watched the ships around him and his Snake Pit Fighters disperse. As he turned his head, the mothership had gone. And so had the majority of its underlings.

"What about the stragglers? Should we take them out?" One of the pilots asked.

The lead Snake Pit Fighter smiled, watching the enemy retreat in quick succession. He felt good about how he and his team had performed. Nothing could wipe the smile off his face, not even the thought of engaging with them once again.

He knew that they hadn't seen the last of that particular mothership and its crew. He also knew that they hadn't felt the last of the Snake Pit Fighters wrath and would one by one, feel it burning into their skin. No one messes with Earth or the Galactic Empire, and the sheer arrogance of these people meant only one thing; they needed to be dealt with severely.

"Don't worry about the stragglers, I'm sure we'll be seeing them again, and when we do, let's make sure there's nothing left of their vessels or their damn mothership."

Chapter Five

The Alpha Ship One shook violently as we ducked and weaved our way past the enemy ships. The onboard computer was sounding an alarm off as I tried to regain control of the bucking vessel. I looked to my left and saw the LCD screen on my console warning me of an imminent missile hit. Before I could even react, the alarm stopped all of a sudden. I stared at the LCD screen for a few seconds, confused as to what was going on, but before I could let it sink in any longer, Dale had sidled up beside me and had hit the FTL switch on the dash next to the LCD screen.

"What the hell are you doing? Didn't you hear the alarm? They were firing at us!" I said, about to disengage the FTL when Dale's massive hand stopped me from doing so.

He placed his shovel-like hand on mine and squeezed down gently. Looking at him, I could see that he was serious. For some reason, and I guess it was an obvious reason at that, he didn't want to be hanging around here any longer than necessary. He may have been a big guy, but he was a sensitive soul as well. And the thought of being blown up by the enemy ships around us was causing the poor guy to bust out in a sweat.

"Of course they are trying to shoot us, what else would they be doing? We need to warp, and we need to do it now," Dale said, releasing my hand, half expecting me to hit the disengage switch. But I didn't. I agreed with them. Getting out of here was the only feasible option.

"Everybody, buckle up. This is going to get bumpy," I said, strapping into my harness, leaning my head back slightly, and closing my eyes.

Usually, whenever the FTL switch was hit, it would give the occupants of the ship around ten seconds before warp speed was activated. It was a complicated process, and relied heavily on a clear path for the warping vessel, void of any objects that could get in our way. What the computer would do is calculate our trajectory and our path of travel. If there were any immediate objects in the vicinity that could hinder our warp, then the engines would turn off and we'd go into cruise mode, until we were able to steer ourselves away from the obstructions. But thankfully, the FTL switch was working just fine, the projected interstellar pathway in front of us was clear and before we knew it, the ten seconds was up and we were hitting warp speeds.

"Here goes nothing," Dale said, strapping his harness on just in time.

Everybody was fastened securely, besides from the guy Dale had knocked out earlier, for he was flopping about on the floor, the ship jolting back and forth, spinning him around like a rag doll. Thankfully, he'd survive, only suffering a few bruises. The others next to him, the three dead ones, they'd be fine too if they weren't already past saving. Once we hit maximum warp, I'd jettison the three of them out of the ship. Space would decide what to do with them. The Alpha Ship One only had room for one traitor, and we'd prefer that the traitor was alive so we could extract information from him. You can't interrogate the dead, so the living would have to do.

There was a lot of information to be extracted. Neither of us knew what the heck was going on. One-minute, Teresa and I had been copulating in the unisex changing rooms on Sector Eight, and then the next, we were being invaded by heavily armed humans, humans that belonged to Earth, but for some reason, were fighting against us. So there was definitely a lot of information to be extracted, that was for sure.

The ship stopped shaking so much after a few minutes, and then evened out, as the tail end of the ship descended slightly, leaving the vessel at an even angle, warp drive fully reached, and maximum speeds fully attained.

I looked at the LCD screen on my dash, and saw that we were now Twenty-five thousand miles away from our original position in the Milky Way Galaxy. FTL travel allowed us to go long distances in a short amount of time. But the problem with warp drives and traveling at such speeds was that it couldn't be sustained for too long.

Well, not on a ship like this. Ever since the troubles with the Ursines, the Earth Galactic Empire had stripped my ship of all of its useful mechanisms and engines. Basically, the Alpha Ship One was only able to travel within the Milky Way Galaxy, and couldn't reach any other galaxies nearby. Not even the Andromeda Galaxy, which is a shame, because I just heard that a mysterious planet had been found. Whenever mysterious planets are discovered by Earth, you can bet your bottom dollar that it has something to do with valuable resources on the surface of that planet. Maybe in time Earth would trust the Alpha Ship One crew again, allowing long-haul missions and such, but I didn't think they'd be trusting us for a long while at least.

Not that it made any sense for them not trust us, especially since it was them in the first place that got us into all that trouble. I hadn't forgotten and neither had my crew. They may have paid us off with a million-dollar credits each, but that wouldn't buy my silence. And I hoped one day I'd be able to get one up on them. To get them back for all the trouble they had caused. For the loss of my original crew. They were good people, and didn't deserve the fateful outcome that they had attained. I believe deep down, one day, Pilgrim Tech will pay, but I just wasn't sure which day that would be.

In my ignorance, I hadn't put the two events together yet. The sudden invasion of Sector Eight, and the dogfights between the warring humans in the Milky Way Galaxy, I hadn't put those two things together. I didn't know that there were people out there that felt the same way as me. But then again – I wouldn't be so quick to cause pandemonium or civil war between my own kind. So as far as I was concerned, even with what I know now, and with what you will come to know soon, there are always other ways to accomplish such a thing.

Revolution doesn't necessarily mean spilling the blood of others. A revolution can be sparked by peace, by common knowledge, by common sense, and compassion. Revolution isn't always accomplished by steel, or resources – wealth - money – credits – whatever you want to call it, nor is it sparked off or generated by the blood of others.

Since the dawn of age, and the dawn of man itself, revolution has played an integral part. There was a time where the people could rise up against a government, a government that oppressed them and suppressed their progression. But it doesn't work like that anymore. Too much good has come out of the Earth Galactic Empire. And I wasn't going to play no part in destroying something I sincerely believed in. And that belief consisted of two things; The freedom of moving through space, and the ability to earn a hard and honest wage.

"Looks like we are out of danger, for now," Teresa said, unstrapping herself and standing up.

She then walked toward the three dead guys on the floor. Kneeling down, she started searching their pockets.

"What are you doing?" I said, also unstrapping myself.

"Seeing if these guys have anything interesting on them," Teresa replied, searching all three of them and then standing back up.

"Find anything?" Philip said, kneeling beside her while staring at the three corpses.

"No, they're clean. I say we chuck them out and wake sleeping beauty up over there," Teresa said.

Dale made his way toward her and without saying anything, he bent down and grabbed all three of them at the same time.

He was a massive man, a beast of a man even, but that didn't mean that I wasn't surprised when I saw him manhandle three grown men and drag them toward the poop chute. And that's exactly what he did. Not even breaking a sweat. He loaded each one of them into the tube and then locked them in there. I walked up to where he stood and grinned at my large friend.

"Not an ounce of compassion - just the way I like my gunners," I said, reaching for a button on the wall and hitting it.

A hissing sound echoed through my ears, and then a prolonged sucking sound followed. I watched through the porthole as all three of the bodies floated away into the void of darkness around the ship. Because of the speed we were going at, the three floating bodies didn't hang around for long.

It was a case of *now* you see them, and *now* you don't.

"Well, that takes care of those three, what about him?" Teresa said, pointing at the unconscious fellow on the floor, who looked as if he was about to wake up from his forcibly induced beauty sleep.

"I guess we wake him up and ask him some questions, what do you guys say?" I said, slowly making my way toward the guy on the floor.

I kicked his leg a few times, lightly, but it was just enough to stir him. Bending down, my knees clicking, I got real close to his face, and smiled. As his eyes opened, he flinched. His pupils constricted and his eyes became red. Veiny lines of various configurations stretched across the whites of his eyes. He sat up quickly and shuffled back a few paces.

"What do you want from me?" The guy said, his bloodshot eyes nearly bulging out of his head.

"All we want is some answers. And I think you're the guy to speak to. So, let's stop all of the shenanigans and get down to brass tacks; what were you and your men doing on Sector Eight and why did you want to kill us?"

The man gulped suddenly, his throat must've been dry, and it looked as if he needed a drink. But he wouldn't be getting anything from us until he answered the questions that needed answering.

He stuttered slightly, so I slapped him across the face. It was just a shock tactic, and it did just that, because both him and Dale, who was standing next to me now, looked a little off put by my actions. I suppose I don't come across as the violent type, but when my crew and myself are in danger, I fully rationalize violence. After all, how else am I supposed to survive?

"If I tell you anything, they'll kill me," the guy said, sweat starting to drip down his face.

I rolled my eyes, stood back up, and turned around, my back facing him.

"I don't think you fully understand what I am asking of you. I don't care if the people you work for, or fight with, or whatever you do with - kill you. All I care about is the safety and well-being of me and my crew. You don't factor into this at all. You are our prisoner. And you know what we do with prisoners if they don't talk? We make them talk. So I suggest you get flapping your gums or I'll flap them for you. Understand?"

I turned back around to face him. He was now looking up at me, his eyes watery and wide like a newborn puppy that just crapped on the floor. I could tell that he had remorse in his soul.

I didn't know if he regretted the fact that he was the bad guy in this or if he regretted the fact that he was the bad guy that just got caught. Either way, I was planning on playing on that remorse of his. Because violence is half the battle when it comes to extracting information from someone not willing to give that information to you. If you can find their weakness, then violence isn't always necessary.

But I had a feeling that this guy would be hard to crack. That didn't mean I wouldn't give it a good go though.

***

Commander Korr of the Annex Rebel Fleet was seething in anger. He couldn't quite believe that his plan was falling apart. This whole mission seemed fragile to him. Like the foundations of it was made from wool and yarn. And all it would take was one pull of a loose thread to untie and unravel everything that he had been working for. Things were going just fine before those damn Snake Pit Fighters showed up. Just thinking about them made his blood boil. And the very fact that he had to retreat wasn't making the matter any more bearable.

If he and his people; the Annex Rebel Fleet, were going to win this thing, then they would need to remain steadfast in their resistance against Pilgrim Tech and its subordinate slaves, the humans of Earth. Running away at the first sign of danger wasn't going to win him any battles. But Commander Korr wasn't an idiot. The Commander was wise, wise beyond his young years, especially since most of the men he would be fighting against, the ones at the top just like him, the suits of Pilgrim Tech, were in their fifties and sixties. Years and years of experience had seeped into their wrinkly and haggard skin. While Commander Korr himself was fresh-faced - yet he held a secret weapon.

And that was a fiery passion in his heart. A passion that he planned on transforming the world with. Earth could no longer be governed by such corrupt immoral powers. There needed to be a revolution, and Commander Korr and his men were that revolution.

The men and women fighting for Pilgrim Tech may have won the first battle, but the Commander was aware of the bigger picture at hand. And that picture was a messy picture. Like dirty watercolors smudged on the canvas of life, this battle was not all that it seemed.

And even though the Commander and his men had retreated, they had learned something valuable from this excursion. They had learned that Pilgrim Tech was scared. They were frightened of the change that the Annex Rebel Fleet represented. It was a change that would affect everybody on Earth. A change that would right the wrongs of the past and divert Earth's and mankind's progress into a new era. An era where everybody was equal. Where everybody had the power to change things beyond their previous reach.

And change was very much the mantra of the Annex Rebel Fleet. But to enforce that change, and to usher in their vision of a new era, there would need to be blood spilled.

Battles would need to be won. Men would need to be cut down to nothing. And authority figures would need to be destroyed. But before any of that could happen, Commander Korr and his men needed to let Pilgrim Tech know what they were in for.

"Sir, unfortunately the unidentified ship warp-drived away from us before we could intercept it with a missile. One of the Snake Pit

Fighters shot down the missile, and the ship got away. I was able to get a better scan of the ship and picked up the soldier identification number emanating from the signal within the vessel. They have four of our men, three of them are dead. Their identification chips are pronouncing them as KIA. As for the remaining soldier on board, life signs suggest that he is fit and healthy. I'm not sure what they want with him, but I fear that they may be able to extract valuable information if they press him hard enough," X-O Zutor said, standing next to Commander Korr as he surveyed his schematic map of the battlefield.

The holographic map revealed that the Snake Pit Fighters had also retreated, along with the majority of the Annex Rebel Fleet. Most of the ships, his ships, were warp driving away from the battlefield, back to their headquarters. They had set up base on a far planet on the fringe of the Milky Way Galaxy, but the planet wasn't known to the people of Earth or Pilgrim Tech. The reason that the planet had remained a secret was because it had been cloaked with an invisibility device.

It had once existed to Earth and its astronomers, most likely as a star, a star that comes to its supernova end, but now, now it was their home base. A base that was far away from Earth and its surrounding planets, but close enough to mount a sizeable attack, an attack that would be effective - they wouldn't have enough time to see them coming – and that was the idea.

"Look, I'm aware of the circumstances regarding the man on the ship and the missile that missed that ship. I'm not stupid, I was standing right here watching as it happened. You may be my right-hand man, but I don't need a play-by-play commentary on the battle. I can use my own eyes, eyes that can see just as well as everybody else's. So I suggest that you drop the act, stop playing Star Trek, and do something useful. Get Admiral Thisk on the line. We need to clear a few things up," Commander Korr said, his scathing remarks making X-O Zutor's face flush beet red.

"Yes sir, right away," his second-in-command said, ignoring the hot flushes that were causing him to sweat profusely.

And even though he'd just been chewed out in front of the majority of their crew, he knew that this operation was causing a tremendous strain on the Commander. A strain that most of the Annex Rebel Fleet staffers were feeling. But unfortunately for X-O Zutor, some people are better at suppressing their feelings than others.

The Commander wasn't one to suppress anything.

"I've requested the linkup, according to the servers, they have received our request. I'm awaiting their response," X-O Zutor said, looking down at the computer tablet in his hands.

The others waited with bated breath around him. Most of them were anxious. Anxious to hear what Earth and Pilgrim Tech thought of their posturing so far.

"They've accepted Sir, patching you in," X-O Zutor said, swiping at the screen and projecting his tablet to the big monitor so everybody else could see.

A few seconds passed and then a static image appeared on the big screen, which everybody on board was now gawking at. The static image was the insignia of Pilgrim Tech, and below that insignia there was some writing flashing every few seconds. The writing simply said "connecting". The Commander found himself staring at the flashing word, the image beginning to ingrain itself into his retinas, but then the flashing stopped and the static image disappeared.

Now the screen showed an uneasy looking man staring directly into the lens of the camera in front of him. His eyes were moist with emotion. And his hair was damp with sweat. He stared at the screen and then attempted a gratuitous smile. But the smile spoke a thousand truths to the Commander, and within those thousand truths was the one greater truth. And that was the fact that Admiral Thisk was scared.

The Annex Rebel Fleet had managed to rattle the cage of Pilgrim Tech, a cage filled with exotic birds of prey. Birds of prey that had ravaged the scorched lands of Earth, biting and chewing at the carcasses of human progression. And now that that cage was firmly rattled, it was time to crush the structure with the birds inside it.

"I take it that you were impressed with our display of aggression and formidable force?" Commander Korr said, breaking out into a smile, a smile that did nothing but rattle the Admiral even more.

But Thisk tried his best to put his game face on, but there was no fooling the Commander or his men. They could see straight through Admiral Thisk's facade. And it did nothing but sicken the Commander, sicken him that this so-called leader of men was quaking in his boots. Where was his spine? Where were his balls? Where were his damn guts?

"You put it into words so perfectly, Commander. As you said, what you just did was definitely a show of aggression and formidable force. But what you don't seem to understand is that humanity and the people on our wonderful planet can see through your villainous acts. You do not scare me Commander. And your fleet of terrorists do not scare the people of Earth. If anything, you make me sad. I have pity for you and your men. You are leading lives of treasonous redemption. And even though you go against your own people and your own planet, your quest for redemption will never be fulfilled. We outnumber you Commander. We outgun you and your men. And believe me when I say this; we outsmart you too. There will be no victory on your part. There will only be sorrow and death. So, I suggest that you retreat back to wherever you came from, and stay there. Because if you return, you will be destroyed. And destruction is something that humanity has always been very good at," Admiral Thisk said.

The Commander stood there on deck, staring at the screen, contemplating his response. He had assumed that the Admiral had been shaken up by their very presence, and his cage had been firmly rattled. And even though he still stood by his original assumption, another thought had crossed his mind. What if the Admiral was so frightened that he did something stupid? It wouldn't be the first time that a leader of men had overreacted, and overplayed his cards. It happened regularly in the past. The last thing he wanted to do was cause the complete and utter destruction of the people on Earth.

The Commander's quarry wasn't with the innocent; it was with the government that overburdened them. Deep in his mind, he had flashes of terror erupting within the depths of his brain. Terror brought on by the established government in response to the Annex Rebel Fleet's attempt at a revolution. He didn't want the people of Earth to suffer at the hands of the government some more. But he couldn't allow Pilgrim Tech or its leaders to know of his compassion toward his fellow man. All they would do is use it against him. And the Commander was aware that it wouldn't take a lot to stop him in his tracks. If the people of Pilgrim Tech decided to threaten the people of Earth with mass extinction, then the Annex Rebel Fleet would most likely cease its operations. But he wasn't going to tell Admiral Thisk that.

He wanted the Admiral to think of him as a villain. A villain that wanted nothing more than to overthrow the government.

It's not uncommon for the rich at the top to be so blinded by their own success that they assume that everybody wants to be just like them. And he wouldn't be surprised if Earth thought that the Annex Rebel Fleet were motivated by money. In this case, the Commander had no issues with letting them assume that. They could think what they liked. But that wouldn't stop the wrath of the Annex Rebel Fleet from crashing down on everyone percenter on planet Earth.

"Admiral, you can continue to think your thoughts of treason and redemption. But don't you dare assume that we are just common terrorists out for mass blood and mass wealth. For we are more than that, and I think you are fully aware of our reasons. All you have to do is look deep inside of your heart, somewhere beneath the dark, putrid, black ooze that coats your soul, dig deep down within that, past the vile wretchedness that is your personality, and then maybe you will be enlightened as to what our cause is truly about.

"But don't boggle your mind with such trivial matters. For there is much more to think about. You shall become aware of our reasoning's in time. But for now, I would just like you to focus on staying alive. Because believe me, Admiral, your life is very much in danger," Commander Korr said, breaking out into a maniacal laugh, and waving goodbye at the screen.

The Admiral was about to retort when the Commander cut the feed. His message had been sent. He wanted Pilgrim Tech to fear the unknown. And messing with their heads was very much a part of Commander Korr's grand plan. A plan that was so complex and so well thought out that even he didn't quite understand it.

But he did understand this; the preservation of Earth and its people was the only reason he was willing to go to war with such unadulterated evil like Pilgrim Tech.

***

I swing my fist back, clenching it hard, and then extend it forward, hitting the prisoner on the jaw. The sound of the punch was loud and foreboding. There was a crunch and then a crack as the prisoner spat some blood out onto the deck. He was on his knees and I was standing over him while Dale was restraining him. I continued to land blow after blow on the mysterious intruder. As I said before, I'm not usually a violent man. But for some reason, the idea of this man prowling on my ship, along with his Three amigos, waiting for us to board the vessel with the sole intention of killing us, was angering me beyond belief.

What right did this man have in taking the lives of my fellow Sector Eight dwellers? What right did these guys have in invading the space station and murdering everyone on it? What were their true intentions behind this? And why in the hell were they dogfighting against our own planet's defenses?

These were not aliens. These were human beings, just like us. And ever since I could remember, human beings were supposed to stick together. Fighting was something of the past. It wasn't something that we did anymore. We were more intelligent than that. We saw the world for what it was, and that was a peaceful safe haven for our species. Species that have worked incredibly hard to get to the top of space exploration, and inter-galactic relations.

Humanity was a leader in the solar system, and in the Galaxy. We were a leader that others looked upon for guidance. And if we couldn't even control our own people, then what future did we have? All of our progress was about to be ruined by a ragtag group of misfits, misfits that wanted to cause nothing but death and despair to their very own species. And men like that, men like the man kneeling below me, blood oozing out of the mouth, didn't deserve any compassion. Violence was the only answer I could summon against such a callous being.

"Tell me the meaning of this! Tell me why you are doing this! You will not leave this ship alive if you do not answer my questions," I said, swinging my fist back once again and landing another hard punch on the intruders face.

But he was a hard nut to crack. And even though I'd been doing nothing but cracking his face with my knuckles, he didn't want to divulge any information to me. He hardly whimpered when I'd hit him. And if he wasn't crying for help, I didn't think he'd be crying for mercy either.

He was cut from a different fabric; I'd seen it before. He was obviously army, or ex-army. Men that were used to pain. Men that were not averse to it. Men that enjoyed the idea of dying an honorable death. And in silence, there was mostly honor. But not when that silence impeded the rightful defense of innocent people.

So I was determined to get through that wall of silence, even if it meant spilling his blood all over the place. Did that make me any better than him? Probably not. But the funny thing about being human is, there's no escaping the need to inflict violence on one another. Everybody has their reasons, and everybody stands by them.

Does that mean that everybody is right? Or does that mean that we've been wrong since day one?

"Tell us what you know," I said, about to lay another hard punch into him when Dale decided to let him go and pull me aside.

"I don't think he's going to talk anytime soon, Capt. Flynn. Maybe violence isn't the answer, maybe we just need to talk some sense into him," Dale said, patting me on the shoulder while giving me an understanding look.

I guess even he was shocked at the lengths I was willing to go to in getting answers. But at the end of the day, these people tried to kill Teresa and I. And I'd had enough of my own people trying to kill me. First Pilgrim Tech had hung my crew and myself out to dry. Sold us to the Ursines – sold us down the river... and then the damn Ursines attempted to trick us into doing their dirty work.

And now, now a new set of humans were trying to kill us. Either I'd been a complete asshole in another life, or the Alpha Ship One had the worst luck in the world, but I was starting to get fed up with it all. I'd done nothing to nobody. Yet everybody had done something to me. It was about time I did something back. But I decided to heed Dale's suggestion. Violence wasn't getting through to this man. But I was determined to get through to him, even if it meant leveling with the enemy. Not that there was much leveling to do. But maybe my past experiences with Pilgrim Tech could earn me some sort of favor with him. Maybe he'd see some sort of kinship with me, a fellow man trodden on by the superior might of the government. But then maybe I was just destined to be trodden on by all types of humanity…

"You're obviously a man of hard exterior and firm beliefs. I can understand your hatred toward Pilgrim Tech, and maybe that's why you decided to attack Earth. And if I'm being honest, I don't really hold it against you. The only thing I do hold against you and your people is the very fact that you tried to kill Teresa and I. Teresa means a lot to me. She's the only one I've got left, no thanks to the people of Earth. And let's not forget, you boarded my ship, a ship that I have flown for the government, a ship that I have paid my dues in, a ship that has protected the interests of our planet and our civilization. And you dare try and take that away from me. You dare try and take away my girl, my crew and my life?" I said, walking up toward the prison on the floor, who was now looking up at me, blood dribbling out of his mouth, and a scowl on his face.

"You don't know anything. You act like you're the righteous one here, and I'm the common thief, trying to take away your all-so-innocent-lives. But you seem to misunderstand the fact that no human is innocent. And no life is safe. We live in a society where we are told we are greater than the Universe. That we mean more than the Universe. That we are the most significant life forms in the Galaxy. Hogwash! We aren't shit. And it's about time that you open your eyes, Capt. Flynn, and realize that this isn't about you. And it's hardly about Pilgrim Tech. It's about something crater. Something greater that you will never understand because you are firmly locked into the social belief that you mean something.

"The day that you realize that you are merely a speck within the sands of time, is the day that you will be on the same wavelength as me. So stop trying to get into my head, because you don't even possess the ability to get into your own," the prisoner said, still staring at me, but this time his scowl had turned into a smile. I guess he was proud of his little speech. And I guess I was intrigued.

"Is the idea behind your attack so righteous that you cannot even bear to tell me? Or is it the fact that you don't actually know why you do the things you do, and the only thing that motivates you is the same thing that motivates all of us, and that's survival. It's all we humans are good at. And maybe you see the world differently from me, granted I can never understand and will never understand the reasoning behind any act of terrorism, but I ain't stupid. I ain't a fool. I understand that we as humans are complex and have different beliefs. But I will never use those beliefs to commit acts of violence upon innocent lives," I said.

The man on the floor tried to stand up. Dale rushed over toward him, and was about to subdue him when I signaled him to stop.

"Let him stand," I said.

Dale did as I asked. He stepped back, and watched as the man struggled to his feet.

The prisoner was swaying from side to side, attempting to regain his balance. And after a few seconds, he composed himself, and raised his head up high. In his mind I guess, this was a victory. He was standing face to face against the opposition. An opposition that had repeatedly beaten him for the last forty minutes.

But I saw things differently. This wasn't a show of force from him, nor was it a show of bravado. This was merely a show of intelligence. As I had been attempting to level with him, now he was leveling with me. For I was standing, and now so was he. We were equals again. And maybe, if we were both equals, in his mind, just maybe I would understand him better. I got the feeling that he was trying to convince me of something. And even though he hadn't spoken since standing, his defiance spoke whispered words to me.

"Now that you're standing, you can tell me the reason behind your attack," I said, moving slowly toward him.

Teresa and Philip were watching from the sidelines, the both of them leaning against the rattling tin wall of the vessel. The ship was on autopilot, and was cruising at a safe speed. The deck was eerily quiet as I awaited the man's response. But I couldn't shake the fact that death had occurred on this deck far too many times now.

A month ago, me and my crew had fought for our right to survive on this deck. We had taken out two Ursines, and I myself had killed one of them. But now, now there was a man on that same deck, a man that had tried to kill me. But I couldn't help but feel that maybe the idea of another living being dying on my ship would curse it to a life of damnation. I wanted nothing but to live a peaceful life. But something was telling me that peace would never be found on board the Alpha Ship One.

"None of you will ever understand the true cause of the Annex Rebel Fleet. But some things aren't meant to be understood. Some things are just meant to happen."

I stood there, staring at the prisoner, shaking my head.

"Instead of talking in riddles, why don't you man up and tell me the truth!" I said, Dale still standing behind the prisoner, watching him intently, just in case he tried to make a move on me. But I was doing the same. I was more than prepared to defend myself once again.

"You think I'm talking in riddles? This isn't a game Capt. Flynn. This is the end. The end of a game that humanity has been playing for centuries. A game of dominance. A game of Monopoly. A game where all the cards have been counted. A game that is in favor of violence and tyranny. It's a game that humanity can never win, because there are no winners in the end. But it is also a game that we, the Annex Rebel Fleet are going to put an end to. Captain Flynn, are you going to sit idly by and watch as we tear the fabric of society apart, or are you going to join us in ending this game once and for all?"

A wave of confusion washed over me, confusion at what he was suggesting. How would I join them? And why would I join them? They tried to kill me. They tried to kill my crew. And as far as I was concerned, this was no game. I don't play with the livelihood of my crew. The fact that he was suggesting that this was all fun and games was making me seethe inside. But I held my anger in and took a deep breath before I answered his call to arms.

"I'm not a kid, I gave up playing games a long time ago. I'm not interested in playing no games here son, this is grown-up shit, and I hope you understand just how serious me and my crew are before you go writing checks your fleet can't cash," I said.

Chapter Six

The men and women standing in the operations room were nervous. Big screens around them projected the carnage that the Annex Rebel Fleet had left behind. To most of the men and women standing in that room, it came as a surprise when they learned that the Annex Rebel Fleet had managed to take out around twenty of their ships. When they came to know how many they'd managed to take out themselves, the nerves they were feeling soon soured and were turned into pure despair instead.

A lot of them were flabbergasted at the fact that the Annex Rebel Fleet had even managed to graze one of their ships, let alone destroy twenty of them. But this was war, and make no mistake about it, the people in this operations room knew the severity of this campaign.

And the reason they knew the severity of this encounter was simple; they had been expecting the rebels to attack. In fact, it had been common knowledge that they were forming some sort of an offensive against the people of Earth and its armies. But a lot of them had thought that maybe the Annex Rebel Fleet were operating on pipedreams alone, so it came as a sort of surprise that they managed to fare so well against their men.

The operational leader stood in the middle the room, surveying his men as they worked tirelessly in front of their terminals. Most of the people working in their terminals had image grabs of the Sector Eight space station above Earth. And within those image grabs was the destruction of that station. It'd been completely destroyed by the Annex Rebel Fleet, and will most likely cost Earth and its people billions of credits to restore. Not that money motivated the people in the operations room, but it was certainly an eye-opener. It was after all the first time in nearly two centuries where civil strife had fallen upon the planet and its people.

Many of the people working for Earth and its government never thought they would see the day where humanity would turn back the hands of time to an era where people killed one another when they disagreed on political or religious means. It was a time that many wished never happened, but unfortunately, history has a habit of repeating itself. And for the operational leader, as he stood in the middle of that room, still surveying his men and women at their terminals, working tirelessly to try and pinpoint the current location of the Annex Rebel Fleet, a sorrowful frown draped his face.

It was no secret, he was depressed. Depressed that it had come to this. The whole point of his operational team was to avert any potential threats against Earth and its people. And he had failed. They had failed. And in the eyes of Pilgrim Tech, his bosses, he knew that he didn't stand much chance of keeping his job. Let alone his life. But he had a duty to uphold. And his duty would only cease to be at the forefront of his mind when he took his last breath. He was determined to take down the Annex Rebel Fleet. Determined to make sure Earth has the last laugh. But truth be told, there wouldn't be much laughing going on when everything came to an end.

"You okay sir?" Somebody said, making the operational leader tilt his head to the left. Standing next to him was one of his interns. A pretty young thing. Fiery red hair and bright blue eyes. She had a concerned look on her face. The operational leader couldn't quite pinpoint the look, part of him thought that it was infatuation, and another part of him thought it was sheer sorrow for his bad luck. He didn't want pity from anybody. Even if she was the prettiest woman he'd ever seen. There was still an air of professionalism around him, and he wanted to keep it that way.

"Yes, I'm fine Maddie. Just a bit taken back by this whole ordeal. I mean, we knew they were coming, but I just didn't expect them to be so damn good," the operational leader said, tilting his head back toward the front, still surveying his team as they worked hard.

In his mind, he was trying to come to terms with what his next course of action would be. But deep down, he knew that any action taken against the Annex Rebel Fleet would have to be violent. It was the only way to defeat them. To stop them in their tracks before they succeeded in their ultimate goal of disrupting the government and its operations.

Maddie looked at her boss and felt a pang of pity for him. She could tell that all of this went way above his and her pay grade. The fact that an attack had happened meant that her team and her boss had failed the system. And she could only imagine what consequences they would face. But she wasn't stupid, she knew that this was still reversible. They knew things after all. Things that could work against the Annex Rebel Fleet.

"Sam, everything will be alright. You'll see, we'll sort this out in the nick of time, and when we do, they'll be calling us heroes," Maddie said, trying to reassure her boss.

Sam smiled back at her, but remained stern at the same time. He didn't dare look her in the eyes. He was far too emotional to feel confident within himself. He didn't want to show his true feelings. These were dangerous times, and he couldn't risk letting his feelings get in the way.

He was a man of action, and actions speak louder than words. And feelings are passive.

They hold no truths, and they speak no lies. They are figments of the human imagination. Figments that cause confrontation among others. And it is those feelings that he had to flush out if he was going to remain in control. And control was very much the only thing that Sam cared about. For he had lost everything else, and control was all he had left.

"Get Pilgrim Tech on the phone. I have a proposition to make," Sam said, staring into the void as he thought about the many lives that were about to be ruined. People were going to die. There was no question about it. But who would suffer the most casualties?

The people of Earth? Or the people trying to destroy it?

***

The Commander of the Annex Rebel Fleet took his hands off the controls and breathed a sigh of relief. His ship was now safely back on the rebel planet. The same planet that was cloaked and hidden from the people of Pilgrim Tech and Earth. If only they could see the sheer size of the Annex Rebel Fleet, then maybe they wouldn't be playing games with him. At least that's what Commander Korr thought to himself. He thought that maybe if they were aware of the sheer danger they were in, then just maybe they wouldn't be so quick to fight back.

Just maybe they'd take into consideration the sheer scale of destruction that the Annex Rebel Fleet was capable of. For they were capable of a lot of destruction. Ultimate destruction. And the very idea that a rebel militia could tear planet Earth in half was unthinkable fifty years ago. But times change. People's guards go down. Earthlings start to trust each other once again. They don't think twice about loving their brother or forgiving their neighbor.

They see the good in everybody.

But the Commander knows that there is only so much good on Earth, and very little of it comes from his fellow human beings. And while Pilgrim Tech were obsessing over interstellar domination, he and his people, a very select few at first, were strategizing and coming up with ways to make the world a better place.

For a very long time, the Annex Rebel Fleet were focused on peaceful protest. They planned on voicing their opinions to Pilgrim Tech, and maybe causing some sort of divide between the citizens of Earth and its masters. But Commander Korr knew that Earth and its people, including the government that held it down, would not be so quick to listen. People had changed. People were no longer interested in revolution, or their rights. They had been brainwashed into thinking that monetary goods were the be-all-and-end-all of existence.

For many years, centuries even, Earth had slowly but steadily conditioned its people to appreciate the material things in life. And once Commander Korr could see that the people of Earth could not be moved or persuaded by pursuits of righteousness, he knew that the only way that his rebel alliance could make a mark on its own planet was by showing force.

After all, force – violence – destruction – physicality, was the only language that the people of Earth understood. But once they became knowledgeable on the rebel fleet's political agenda, then maybe – just maybe, they could gain some sort of stronghold within the political system.

The Annex Rebel Fleet aren't terrorists. Pilgrim Tech are the terrorists. They terrorize the banks, and the people that own houses on Earth, paid with money loaned to them at high-interest rates, just so they can die in debt.

Pilgrim Tech monopolies everything. They are a stain on the progress of humanity. For there is much more to life than the commercialization of space. Back when interstellar travel became a reality, Commander Korr and his people had a vision where the knowledge of humanity's existence would be sought after. But instead, interstellar travel had been used to monetize certain resources and certain planets. And for his people, his alliance, rebel or not, that was not good enough.

And now the Commander found himself back on his secret planet. A planet that was teeming with rebel fighters. Hundreds of thousands of men and women that were just like him. Men and women that could see the absolute lack of human empathy back on Earth. Rebels that wanted nothing but peace and prosperity for their family members on their home planet. But the only way that the Annex Rebel Fleet could gain any sort of peace was through violence, unfiltered violence toward their oppressors.

The Commander hoped that Pilgrim Tech would see the error of its ways. And even though, hypothetically, Pilgrim Tech outnumbered the Annex Rebel Fleet, they were just men in suits. And men in suits did not take arms up against their enemies. They use and manipulate the people that they rule over instead. And it is those people that suffer. It is their families that grieve.

And it is now that the Annex Rebel Fleet will put an end to human capitalism and usher in a new dawn for all of mankind.

But before any of that can come into effect, much planning needed to be done. And even though the Commander already had the blueprints for his *do or die* mission, there were still certain pawns on the chessboard that needed to be moved forward. Though the Commander preferred cards, and saw this very much like a game of poker, sometimes proficiency in both games can come in handy.

The Commander stared at his controls in front of him, and watched as the ship's power systems fluctuated back to idle mode. His engines were cooling off, and so was his anger. The Commander knew that he would need to keep a firm grasp on his emotions if he was going to succeed in this mission. But it was hard for the Commander not to get emotional when it came to his dream.

A dream that he'd had for many years. And that dream was simple; take the world back and share it equally among men and women.

"Commander, you are needed at the Pavilion," X-O Zutor said, approaching the Commander with caution, for he looked as if he was deep in thought.

Commander Korr turned around and faced his right-hand man. Both men remained silent for what seemed like an eternity, but was more than likely just a few seconds. The realization of what they were doing was slowly sinking in. They were really doing it. They were really moving forward. Both of them could hardly believe it. Everything was happening so fast. But there was no mistaking the fact that the two of them had accomplished something great.

Something great that would change the course of humanity forever.

"Lead the way," Commander Korr said, following his right-hand man out of the ship and onto rebel soil.

The planet was barren. It held a kinship to Mars. The ground was red and the rocks were rusted by the sun. But this particular planet didn't share the same hostile conditions as Mars. The atmosphere was comfortable. None of the rebels needed oxygen tanks to walk on the surface. The planet's atmosphere was breathable, and hypothetically, the planet could support human life if need be.

But that's not why the Annex Rebel Fleet were using it. None of them lived on it. The planet was used for one thing and one thing only; and that was storing their war machines. It was their so-called launchpad for their war. Their troops were stationed on the planet, and rotated themselves back and forth between Earth and here, as to not arouse suspicion with the people that knew them back home. But now that their plan was in motion, there would be no more going back to Earth to keep up appearances.

The Annex Rebel Fleet were now permanently stationed on this planet. And Commander Korr had no problems with that whatsoever. They had planned this for many years. So many years in fact, some of the founding members of the Annex Rebel Fleet had died long ago. But there were provisions on this planet, provisions that would keep them fed and hydrated until the time was right to strike. Not that the Commander thought he and his men would be spending much more time on this planet.

The wheels were now turning, and there was no stopping this train. The line stretched all the way toward earth, and the final stop was victory. Commander Korr and his men couldn't wait much longer, the excitement was too great. But there were a few final intricate details to sort out. And one of those details was waiting for him in the Pavilion.

The Commander and his right-hand man X-O Zutor walked past various ships that were idle on the red soil. Looking around, canyons and mountains surrounded them. They hadn't wasted much time on this planet, and didn't bother building any buildings or landmarks. All the troops slept onboard their ships. The vessels acted as their temporary homes. Homes that doubled up as war machines as well. The only man-made structure on the planet was the Pavilion.

Its purpose was simple; it acted as the meeting point for all the Annex Rebel Fleet members to talk about certain subjects. Commander Korr and X-O Zutor entered the Pavilion, it lay empty apart from two or three souls standing in the middle, chatting amongst themselves. All the troops were on board their vessels, most likely eating, drinking and sleeping.

But the three souls in the Pavilion spotted the Commander and his right-hand man and ushered the two of them forward. It didn't take long for the Commander to reach the three men who at first he didn't recognize, but then as he got closer, he recognized just fine. The Pavilion's many chairs and tables were packed away. The place looked desolate, but the Commander knew that if he was being summoned, it must be important.

So he didn't bother with pleasantries, he just stood there expectantly, waiting for whatever news he was about to receive. The three men standing in front of him looked a little nervous, but that was only because he was the Commander – their leader – and most men get nervous in the presence of greatness.

"Sir, we have an update on the mole's progress," one of the men said, looking the most nervous of all.

He wore army fatigues, the same fatigues that everybody else wore, but he had a special patch on his right arm. He was one of the chairmen of the Pavilion. His job was to officiate meetings between the various leaders of the Annex Rebel Fleet. Commander Korr was at the top of the table. But that didn't mean that the others weren't just as important as him.

They were a team after all. And teams work together. The last thing that he wanted to do was fall into the same trap that Earth did. Pilgrim Tech was a group of elitists. In the Annex Rebel Fleet, every man was equal. High-ranking positions were given to men of experience, but all men were equal when it came to their place in the rebel fleet.

"How is the mole doing? Is he any closer to succeeding?" Commander Korr said, fiddling with his hands a little as he cracked his knuckles.

"Yes sir, I just had word back from him. Apparently, he's only hours away from accomplishing his objective. He said that the attack has scattered the officials back on Earth. And it seems as if the panic that we have caused is working in our favor, just as you predicted," the man said.

Commander Korr nodded, a wry smile coming across his face.

"So the president of Pilgrim Tech should be getting a visit from the mole soon. Let's hope that he doesn't put up much of a fight, because I want him alive. Once we get him in our custody, then we'll be that much closer to a checkmate," Commander Korr said, the smile on his face becoming bigger as he thought about what they were about to do.

It had never been done before. A high-ranking member of Pilgrim Tech was about to be kidnapped. And once he was kidnapped, then they would hold all the power in the world.

Once that power was theirs, they'd be that much closer to victory.

***

After around twenty minutes of silence, I had decided to move back toward my flight chair. Sitting back down on it, I could feel my back muscles relaxing as the tension dissipated off my shoulders. I cracked my neck a few times, trying to get the nicks out of my knotted spine.

The others had fallen silent. Dale was standing next to the equally silent prisoner, keeping an eye on him. Teresa had been quiet throughout most of the ordeal. If I had to guess the reason for her silence, it was most likely due to her replaying the memory of putting a knife into the back of that woman earlier. I know I was doing the same.

As for Philip, he was also quiet. I guess all of this was a lot for him to take in, as it was for me. We were after all just getting over the fact that we had been allowed back into the inner circle of Earth. We were no longer traitors, even if Pilgrim Tech had been the actual traitors to begin with, I couldn't help but sympathize with the Annex Rebel Fleet a little. From what the prisoner had already told me, I could understand their frustrations. It seemed as if these particular rebels had the people of Earth's best interest at heart. But that didn't mean that I trusted them.

So far, all he'd mentioned was that Earth would pay for what they had done to the other members of the Galactic Empire. And as far as I was concerned, I could relate. After all, I had been complicit in the act of exterminating the Ursines. And even though the Ursines had wanted my people dead, I still felt a certain empathy for their plight.

But empathy and sympathy and all the words that end with the letter 'Y' weren't going to bring about peace in these turbulent times. Earth had made its bed and now it had to lie in it. And the same went for the Annex Rebel Fleet. They had attacked a human settlement and if I knew Pilgrim Tech like I thought I knew them, then they wouldn't be getting away with it.

I wouldn't be surprised if the leaders of the so-called Annex Rebel Fleet were strung up in the public square, back on Earth, back at the capital, in front of all of the peasants and underlings of high society. They would be made an example of. And it was an example that Pilgrim Tech would enjoy instilling. They were not afraid of getting their hands dirty. But then again, maybe I was giving them too much credit? Who's to say that the Annex Rebel Fleet didn't have a chance in this? Who's to say that they couldn't win?

Maybe they had all the chance in the world? But let's not forget that we aren't talking about just the world here, or at least not just planet Earth, but we are also talking about the Galaxy. The Universe. And peppered throughout them both were many humans.

Human civilization had expanded exponentially. And there wasn't a single planet, hostile or otherwise, that hadn't seen the footprint of an Earth national on their own soil.

This was much bigger than us. And I was curious to know what their plan was when it came to the other expats out there in deep space. There were private armies in most regions of the Galaxy. And it wouldn't take much for those armies to come trundling back, and fight the good fight for the men and women that had made them so rich years ago.

"I see you contemplating your situation Capt. Flynn, but I don't hear you asking the right questions. So far, all you have been interested in is the *why's* and the *how's* of the matter. But hasn't it occurred to you that maybe there is much more to this than just that?" The prisoner said, wiping some blood off his face.

I didn't bother looking at him. I was fine with just hearing his voice. Maybe that's what it would take to get him to talk. Maybe my reluctance to smash his face into a million pieces had proven useful after all.

At first, I kicked myself for being weak and not having the stomach to get the job done. Because if it was me on the other side, and these savages had me prisoner, I bet they wouldn't hesitate in carving my face up. But I guess I had something that they didn't, and that something was *understanding*. I understood my fellow man more than most did. And from my many years of understanding other men, I have come to the conclusion that it is best to shy away from unnecessary bloodshed when possible. And maybe it's that shyness toward violence that was making the prisoner talk right now…

I wasn't going to ruin it by opening my mouth, though.

"You hear me Capt. Flynn? I can see your eyes moving, the cogs in your mind are spinning away. But unfortunately for you, this isn't the sort of thing that you can just win via mental capacity or intelligence alone. This is the sort of thing you can only win by joining us – the eventual winners of this whole thing," the prisoner said, wiping more blood off his face.

"Joining you? You want me to join you? You tried to kill me not too long ago. You tried to kill my crew. Yes - I am a forgiving man, and I hold a great deal of respect for the lives of others, but don't mistake that for weakness. If I had half the chance, I'd gut you like a pig. Only a pig would shit on its own doorstep after all. And you have done a lot of shitting, haven't you? This whole mission has been one massive pile of excrement – aimed solely at the men and women that have sheltered you, and made you into a citizen. Earth is your home. You're desecrating it with your frivolous pursuit of happiness – happiness that you plan on attaining by killing innocent people. But once this is over, and you lie dying in a pool of your own blood, along with the people you thought were your brothers in arms, you won't be happy, because there is no way that happiness can be found with the sword, the gun or the fist."

The prisoner started to laugh. It was a surreal sight. Half his teeth were knocked down his throat, yet he'd found something to smile about.

"You talk as if you are a wise man, Capt. Flynn. But if you were so wise you would see that there is much more to this than you think. You actually think that a group of rebels would attack Earth if it didn't think it could win? Surely you aren't that stupid? We in the Annex Rebel Fleet do not waste our breath when it comes to violence. For when we strike, we strike hard and we strike with purpose. And there is no purpose whatsoever in striking without the firm knowledge that your strikes will count, and your opponent will fall. But you need to focus less on the reasoning behind our violence or the violence itself, and start thinking about the bigger picture at hand Capt. Flynn.

"We have our ways Captain. And our ways are right and just. But you can continue to convince yourself that the people of Earth hold some sort of righteousness of their own. I don't want to get in the way of any fantasies that you may have about your fellow man, but I'm afraid that everything you know about mankind and the human condition is wrong.

"For so many years we have been told that we are special and we hold some sort of significance within this great void of space that surrounds our planet and solar system. But I am afraid that there is nothing significant about us. We are mainly men bound by flesh and greed. There is no Higher Power and there is no righteousness on our planet. We have done so much that is so wrong that I fear we can never get anything right again. But now is very much our chance as a society to wash our putrid streets of the filth that once drenched the alleys around us. And it is you Capt. Flynn and your ship that holds the key to our mission. Why do you think we found ourselves on board your ship?

"It wasn't to murder you Capt. Flynn, it was to recruit you. Why else would we board the starport? What significance does Sector Eight have for us, a rebel fleet, with the sole purpose to destroy, and not to infiltrate? It was to retain your services Capt. Flynn. I understand that your crew and the Alpha Ship One are a ship for hire. And we have the full intent of hiring you for your services. So ask yourself this Captain and fellow crew mates; do you have what it takes to change the world for the better? And I'm not just talking about our world, I'm talking about the worlds that are millions of light-years away from us, worlds that could be allies in a peaceful - yet sovereign alliance. Is that dream so bad? Is it so bad to want peace for the entire Galaxy? The entire Universe? I think not. But then again, you are merely just *Plan A* for us. If you do not wish to partake in our little game, then we have other means of accomplishing our goals," the prisoner said, wiping the last bit of blood off his face.

The whole of the bridge went quiet. Everybody was deep in contemplation. Even Dale was thinking hard about what the prisoner had just said. I caught an uncertain glance from Teresa. She had her doubts. So did I. But I would be lying if I said I wasn't half interested in what the prisoner was saying. I wanted to know more. I wanted to know everything. And if that meant convincing him that I wanted to take part in his little game, as he described it, then so be it. I too could play games.

But I'm pretty sure that there would only be one winner once this was over.

"So tell me then; how are you going to change the world," I said, standing up and walking toward the prisoner, who was still on his knees, looking up at me.

"It's simple really. All I need is one promise from you before I tell you about our plan. Sound good to you?"

I stood there thinking for a few seconds. I then looked at each member of my crew. Philip looked worried. Dale looked transfixed by my stare. And then there was Teresa. She smiled at me. And then nodded. That's when I knew that the game was very much in play.

"What is it that you want me to promise?"

The prisoner stood up abruptly. Dale was about to restrain him when I put my hand out to stop him. Dale nodded at me and then fell back, leaning against the wall of the rattling ship as it warp-drived through the Milky Way Galaxy. I then turned to the prisoner and nodded my head expectantly, waiting for his demands.

"I don't ask you for much, but I ask you of this; when I tell you what I know, please promise me that you'll have an open mind. For this to work, for you to understand what is needed of you and your crew, you're going to need to be as open-minded as possible."

I nodded my head sternly. Open-mindedness was my specialty.

Chapter Seven

Operational leader Sam had been called to the conference room. One minute he'd been on the main floor, surveying his team as they'd worked on their computer terminals, trying to pinpoint the exact location of the Annex Rebel Fleet, and then the next minute he'd been summoned to the dark and dank offices at the top of the building.

The elevators were out, so he had to take the stairs. And after about ten minutes of sweat inducing climbing, he reached the top floor, his forehead covered in a sheet of perspiration, his eyes dry with dehydration and his heart pounding in his chest.

He exited the staircase and walked into a narrow hallway. The hallway was peppered with filing cabinets and paperwork strewn all over the place. Usually, the top floor was a hive of activity. But now it was desolate.

He hadn't seen a single person up there. And from what he could tell, operational leader Sam was definitely alone. Not that he was scared of being alone, but he was definitely scared of being summoned to talk with the bosses. Maddie, who had told him about the conference call, hadn't been specific on what they had wanted from him. But he could guess that it had little to do with praising him, and a lot to do with scaring him.

After all, that is how Pilgrim Tech worked. They relished in the fear of others. Their game plan was simple; use fear to progress. And that is what they did. And they did it well. But the eeriness of the desolate top floor was making Sam feel uneasy. There he was, the leader of the pack, separated from his wolves. He worked better within a team, but the thing is; his team weren't working well with him.

They were failing their mission. And operational leader Sam was aware of their failures. He was probably more aware of their failures than they were. A lot of the people he commanded worked in a bubble. A bubble of security. They turned the blind eye, and thought they were fighting the good fight. They tried to convince themselves that what they were doing was just and right. That without them, without their overlords; Pilgrim Tech, then nothing on this planet could survive.

But Sam knew differently. He knew that in his field lies were a commodity that were traded amongst most well-to-do men. And he had no doubt that they had definitely been lied to. He just didn't know to what extent.

But that didn't matter to Sam. All that mattered was getting through the conference call. And as he walked down another hallway, toward the conference room, he couldn't help but look around in awe at the complete and utter loneliness that surrounded him.

Every office that he passed was empty. Every light was turned off. The hum of the computers was deafening. But he couldn't hear any typing. He couldn't hear any phone calls being made or received. He couldn't hear the usual chatter amongst the workers. All he could hear was his constant heart beating through his chest. The nape of his neck was moist with sweat. His feet felt heavy as they clunked on the carpet. It was as if there was no carpet underneath him. And with every step he took, another deafly crunch echoed through the silence.

The crunching continued as he approached the ominous conference room at the end of the hallway. The wallpaper around him seemed to be peeling, but it was most likely all in his head. For in reality, the place wasn't as scary or desolate as he saw it. Yes, there were no workers working on the top floor, and there was most likely a reasonable explanation for that particular coincidence, but operational leader Sam couldn't help but think he was in a horror movie.

Or this was a hit. An attempt on his life. They were going to kill him. He was sure of it. Why else would all the workers be missing? Why else would there be no one to greet him at the top?

He stopped in his tracks for a few seconds, breathing heavily, his raspy lungs aching against his rib cage. The sweat dripping down his neck had now made its way down his lower back. It was like an ice cube being smudged into his hot skin. And every time a new drip found its way down his lower lumbar, he winced in pain. His eyes were strained, as a one-sided headache ravaged his skull. But he had to remain strong. He couldn't show any weakness.

This wasn't the time to freak out. This wasn't the time to speculate.

He was needed – and had been ordered to attend the conference room. And even though he was a mere meter or so away from the door, staring at the handle, he couldn't help but feel terrified at what lay behind it. A foggy window above the door revealed the darkness inside the conference room. Nobody was there.

At least, nobody was there with the lights on.

He started to panic. He couldn't quite catch his breath. Every time he tried to, he started to choke, as if suddenly, the air around him manifested itself into something physical, something sharp and thick. Something he could swallow and choke on. He closed his eyes, trying to will himself to open the door.

And then he heard it.

A familiar sound. A phone ringing. The ringing phone was coming from within the conference room. It was loud and screeching as he stood there, still trying to find the guts and bravery that he once had. But his guts had long gone, along with his bravery, the day he signed on the dotted line and became a member of Pilgrim Tech. They say that ignorance is bliss; but when he joined the organization, there was no room for ignorance. Knowledge became fear. But he wasn't afraid of the unknown, it was the known that he feared. And the ringing phone in the conference room, locked behind the oak door, only cemented that fear.

Because he knew that once he walked through those doors, and answered that phone, he'd know the true extent of the reason behind him being summoned to the top. And from his experience, knowing Pilgrim Tech's full intentions usually filled the common man with dread.

But Sam couldn't stand there like an idiot, waiting for the phone to stop ringing. He knew that he was being watched. He craned his head up, opened his eyes wide, and saw a security camera staring directly at him.

The light on the camera, inbuilt near the lens, was flashing green. As he moved toward the door, the camera followed him. He cleared the meter between him and the door within a second. Putting his hand on the handle, he slowly but steadily clicked the door open, pushing it until he could see the void of the conference room.

Without hesitating, knowing that they were still watching him, he stepped into the conference room, quickly turning on the lights, trying to act calm, walked up to the table, a large table, usually home to men in suits, sitting around it like the Lords that they were, and approached the ringing phone. The phone was close to the door, so he didn't need to walk around the large table.

He quickly picked it up, cleared his throat, and took a deep breath in.

"Hello operational leader Sam, my name is Agent Six," the voice on the other end of the phone said. Sam's eyes widened - he was talking to an agent and not a boss – and that couldn't be a good thing.

Agents were the backbone of Pilgrim Tech. They were ruthless in their pursuit of the truth. Their sole purpose was to audit and control Pilgrim Tech's subordinates. In all his time within the organization, operational leader Sam had never talked to an agent. He'd heard stories of people that had. Stories of them never returning to the organization again. Stories of them disappearing off the face of the planet.

Off the edge of the Galaxy, even.

"I take it that you know that the fact that I'm calling you means something significant, right?" The Agent said, his voice raspy and gravelly. Operational leader Sam wasn't sure if the man was using a voice changer, or if his voice was that scary naturally.

"Is this about the Annex Rebel Fleet? We are trying our best to pinpoint their location, sir. I know that you have a job to do, but so do I. I don't think I'm much good up here taking phone calls, when I should be down there trying to win us this war," Sam said, surprised of his bravado on the phone. He wanted the Agent to know that he wasn't scared. But in doing so, the choice of words that he'd used, Sam thought that he'd already blown it.

"So you think this is a war?" The Agent asked.

Sam gulped, hoping that it wasn't audible on the phone.

"Well, we were attacked. So I figure that the fact that we were attacked by an enemy force that wants us to disband our operations, while threatening us with violence, means that we are very much at war," Sam said.

"Good, you aren't as stupid as I thought you were. You are right, operational leader Sam. This is war. And in times of war, many great men are needed. Men that can pull their weight and get the job done. The reason I am calling you a simple; you have been an asset to this organization. And we want you to continue to be an asset to this organization. But unfortunately, it seems that during the pressure of this ordeal, your team and yourself have lost your spark. You see Sam, this whole organization runs on spark – mustard – spunk, whatever you want to call it. It runs on it like an engine runs on fuel. When our team members run out of fuel, all burned out and close to crashing, we like to remind them of the reason why they joined our little team."

"Sir, I'm fully aware of the reasons. And I appreciate the phone call, but I can assure you that we have everything under control," Sam said.

There's a moment or two of uncomfortable silence. Operational leader Sam could hear the crackle of the phone against his ear. The Agent was far away. The quality of the call proved that to be a fact. But it felt as if the Agent was right next to him, whispering in his ear. He could feel the man's breath against his neck. The menace in his voice. The monotone decibel of his speech, overbearing against his eardrum.

And then he spoke again.

"I'm ever so glad that you are adamant in completing your mission, operational leader Sam. But the reason I am calling you is to instill a little motivation in you. As I said, this organization runs on spark. And from time to time, we as human beings lose sight of our original goals. These goals are very important to Pilgrim Tech. But we understand, no one is perfect. And we aren't asking you or your team to be perfect. All we are asking you is to remember the cause. To remember the reason why we fight. To remember that we are being attacked by an enemy contingent that wants nothing but destruction for our way of life. And just so you understand what I'm trying to say here operational leader Sam, let me affirm to you of the severity of failing this mission," the Agent said.

Sam closed his eyes, and readied himself for whatever the Agent was about to lay down on him.

"You see Sam, if we lose this fight, and let the rebels win, then we risk losing a lot more than our organization. I cannot guarantee the safety of your family if you continue to lag on this mission. I hope you understand what I'm trying to say to you, operational leader Sam. And if you don't understand, I'm pretty sure that my assumption on the danger of your family will come true," the agent said, his voice sounding a little deeper than before.

Sam opened his eyes, they were moist. Deep down, he'd known what this call would have been about from the start.

"I'll take your silence as a sign that you are fully aware of the situation – and the impact of your possible failure on us all. I hope that I have cleared things up for you. The last thing I want to happen is for our family members to suffer for our sins, Sam. But unfortunately, we live in a world where the sins of the father have to be accounted for," the Agent said, the phone line going dead almost immediately.

Sam stood there, tears in his eyes, heart thumping in his chest and sweat dripping down his face. He stood there for what seemed like an eternity, staring at the emptiness of the room as the threats from the Agent sunk into his psyche. Was his family really in danger? Would they really sink to that level? Or was this all part of the act?

Sam didn't have the answers to those questions, but he did know what he had to do to avoid finding out.

And that was win.

***

There was a mysterious man roaming the offices of the Pilgrim Tech officials. He was a non-descript man. He didn't hold any significant facial features nor did he stand out from the crowd. He was just another suit. Another suit doing his job. A computer tablet in his right hand, a cup of coffee in his left. A drab tie around his neck. Non-designer eyeglasses. No facial hair. No tattoos. No smile. Just a man going about his business. But he had two jobs that day. His first job, and the least important one at that, was to do his duties in the office.

File papers. Attend meetings. Be a part of the chaos. But his second job, the most important one, was a secret one. It was a job that no one in the Pilgrim Tech offices were aware of. And thankfully so, because if they found out about his second job, his most important job, then he probably wouldn't be walking out of that office alive today.

But the man was clever. And being non-descript, he blended in like a chameleon on a tree.

And it was from this tree of life and death that he blended in, just another face in the crowd. He continued with his first job. And for the past few hours he'd been bringing coffee to the other, much more powerful people in suits while they talked about the crisis in the Milky Way Galaxy. He remained quiet as he gave them cup after cup, pretending not to listen, but taking in everything they said.

It wasn't as if he needed to know how they felt. He could see it on their faces. They were scared. And their fear made him happy. For so many years, he'd worked under the fringes of society. And for the majority of those years, he'd been a law-abiding citizen. But the nondescript man became fed up with how the world worked. He'd seen too many good people suffer at the hands of the government. And even though he currently worked for the government, there comes a point when even the most stubborn man loses faith.

But instead of doing what most would do, and quit, he decided to stay along for the ride. And what a ride it was going to be! He knew of men, men that wanted nothing but to overthrow the government on Earth. Men that would stop at nothing to bring the complete and utter destruction of the elite to fruition. And it was with these men that he socialized with, grew to like, grew to trust and above all grew to serve.

It's hard to hold down two jobs at once. But for this non-descript, nonconforming, non-rattled man, having a purpose in life far outweighed the possible dangers of going against the grain. And that was exactly what this man was doing. Smiling to their faces, handing them coffee, holding down a non-descript job to match his nondescript face, just so he could be of use on this very special day.

"Thanks," one of the men in suits sat around the table said as the non-descript man handed the very powerful man a cup of hot steaming Joe.

Out of the eighteen other men that he'd just handed coffee to, this was the only one of them that had said *thank you*. The non-descript man would remember that. He would store that in his memory banks. And when the shit hits the fan, and the men around this table would come to their end, he'd remember that man that said thanks.

He'd die quicker than the rest. It was the right thing to do.

After all, mercy was an important part of war. And this was war. A war from the inside. At least for this man. Pushing his coffee tray out of the meeting room, the non-descript man had a smile on his face. It went against everything he stood for. Smiling was not advisable when you wanted to remain below the surface of life –

bubbling away – waiting for your moment to come to make yourself known. A smile gave away too much too soon to too many people. But seeing that he had his back to the men that he was about to help destroy, he figured that smiling wouldn't hurt much.

"Enjoy your coffee," the nondescript man muttered under his breath, closing the double doors behind him, and retreating into the shadows until the time was right.

Right to strike…

Chapter Eight

After what seemed like a very long time, the prisoner stopped talking. So far, he had made a believable case for himself. He'd tried to convince myself and the Alpha Ship One crew that there was more to this than met our collective eye. That his people, the so-called Annex Rebel Fleet, were an alliance of rebels that held the best interests of Earth and its people at heart.

He told us that their goal was to destabilize the corrupt government that controlled every aspect of our lives. Though what he was saying was far-fetched and borderline treasonous, I couldn't help but sympathize with the idea that he was similar to me. After all, I had been on the end of Pilgrim Tech's hit list once before. They had discarded me like trash. Thrown me away, along with my crew, onto an alien planet. They had marooned me from my people. And above that, they had cost the lives of serving members of my crew.

I didn't know how much more savagery I could forgive. In my mind, I had done enough forgiving as it was. Pilgrim Tech had ruined the lives of many, and I wasn't narrow-minded enough to see them as the good guys. But there are people out there that see things black-and-white. And this particular prisoner was one of those types. He saw Pilgrim Tech as evil. He also saw the people of Earth as suppressed, and oppressed at the same time. He saw them as people that didn't know how to stand up to the elites of the world.

But as I said, not everything is as black-and-white as he says it is. There are many layers to the foundation of society. Some of those layers are blacker than others. And some of them are whiter. But together they form a contingent. A contingent that holds and glues the lives of many.

I didn't know if I was prepared to join the Annex Rebel Fleet, as he had suggested. And I certainly couldn't speak for the majority of my crew. Teresa would probably not want any part of this. Not to mention Philip. The two of them held a simplistic look on life. And after what they had been through on the Ursines planet, all they wanted was a peaceful life.

As for Dale, my longest serving member, and the only surviving member of the originals, he would most likely side with whatever I chose. Dale had a mind of his own, but unfortunately, that mind was easily swayed when it came to following his Captain. All Dale wanted to do was please me. But all I wanted to do was please everybody else.

My solemn silence was interrupted by the prisoner.

"I see that you are thinking long and hard about my proposal. And I don't blame you really. It's a lot to take in. I'm not asking much of you, or your crew. All I want you to do is hear me out. Hear what I have to say. Listen to the facts and digests them. And after all is said and done, whatever decision you make will be one made confidently."

"I've listened to your sales pitch, and I must admit I am intrigued to know more. But that's where me and you differ, prisoner. So far, all you have told me is the fairytale aspect of your rebel fleet. You've told me what you stand for, and what you hope to accomplish. But unfortunately, I need more than that. I need logistics. I need facts. I need numbers. And until you give me what I want, I cannot guarantee that your fate is one of safety. Don't forget that you are still a prisoner of ours. We dispatched of your three amigos earlier, and we won't hesitate in dispatching of you either," I said, sitting in my captain's chair, keeping an eye on the warp drive status screen.

The prisoner was standing in the middle the room now, next to Dale, who was leaning against one of the control desks. Teresa was sitting next to me, and Philip was standing near the double doors that exited the bridge. Everybody was quiet as the prisoner remained standing, a look of defeat on his face.

It was obvious from his facial expressions that he was struggling with the idea of telling me the whole truth. Not that I considered him a liar, but I did consider him a threat. And I'm pretty sure that he considered us dangerous. We had, after all, dispatched of his three friends earlier. And I could tell that the very fact that I had mentioned it to him, had reminded him of the predicament that he was in.

He sighed loudly, and slowly walked toward me. Dale kept an eager eye on him, making sure that he stayed in line. As he made his way toward me, I knew that he was about to give up the goods. His poker face had dropped. And so had his shoulders. They were no longer stern, and he walked like a newborn calf.

A calf that was unsteady on its legs. The only thing missing from this picture was a nurturing mother by its side. He knew he was alone. Alone in this cold, dark world that he found himself in. The Alpha Ship One was my world. I was King. My crew were his tormentors. And he knew very well how much danger he was in. So it was certainly time to give up what he knew.

"Fine, if you really want to know everything, then I guess everything you shall know. But there's something I want you to know. The only reason I haven't been as forthcoming as I would have liked, is because I know my place on board this ship. I am your prisoner. I am in a lot of danger – grave danger. And the big problem is; you want something from me. You want information. Information that I have. It's my way out of this. I know it, and you know it. It would have been stupid of me to not hold back on what I know. They needed to be an understanding between the both of us before I could risk giving up the only thing that's keeping me alive. Don't you agree?" The prisoner said, now standing next to my captain's seat, staring down at me as I looked up at him.

I could tell that he was frightened. But for the first time since he'd opened his mouth, even though it was still covered in blood, I could now tell that he was being sincere. My original idea of beating the living crap out of him to get answers had failed. But my secondary plan of talking him down from the proverbial ledge had worked. I was seconds away from entering the inner circle of the Annex Rebel Fleet. And within that inner circle, there were secrets and facts that I needed to know. Facts that could either help or hinder the Alpha Ship One. I had most likely already made my mind up on whether I was joining the Annex Rebel Fleet or not. And I'm pretty sure the only reason the prisoner had mentioned the possibility of me and my crew joining was to save his own skin.

But I had my own reasons. And maybe it was time that I made them clear.

"Look, prisoner – I don't know your name, nor do I want to know your name. Me and my crew have been beaten, dragged, and thrown all of our lives. We are misfits. We hold no loyalty to nobody. And the fact that you assume that we want to protect Pilgrim Tech is an insult to every member that has ever stepped foot onboard the Alpha Ship One. If you knew who I am, and who my crew are, you would be appalled at the idea that we were even chummy with the government of Earth, let alone working for it.

"So don't waste your breath trying to convince us of your cause. It's a cause that I have held in my heart for many years. It's a cause that the Alpha Ship One stands for on its own merit. We don't need the Annex Rebel Fleet to make us realize the error of our ways. We were clever enough to realize those errors long before your stupid little group formed and wrecked everything. Make no mistake, pal, you have wrecked everything! What makes you think that fighting against the government of Earth is going to save the people on our planet?

"What makes you think that spilling blood is the answer here? What makes you think that I haven't had these fantasies of taking over the world and making it a better place? You think that you are the first person to ever want to rise up against the establishment? Well I'm sorry to break it to you, prisoner, but you aren't the first and you won't be the last. But here's the kicker; if you play your cards right, you may actually have a chance at making your fantasies become a reality. But before you even contemplate spilling any more blood, I need you to promise me that you are serious about your cause," I said, noticing how surprised the prisoner was as he stood next to me, still staring down at me, still bloodied in the mouth.

"I promise. This is real. We've been planning this for years. We have a planet. They don't know about it. But on that planet, we've been amassing weapons – ships – personnel and ammunitions. We can do this. We have the numbers and we have the will. But we need someone on the inside. We've always needed someone on the inside. And that person is you. It's your crew. It's your ship. It has always been your ship. You just didn't know it," the prisoner said.

I blinked a few times, turning toward Teresa and Philip. They had smiles on their faces. It wasn't what I expected. I expected them to be angry. Angry that somebody had been targeting us to be their pawn in their unstructured rebellion.

But it was true what the prisoner had said. It made sense. So far, from what I had heard from him, the so-called Annex Rebel Fleet knew their stuff. But as I said before, I needed to know more.

"So tell me, tell me everything. You say you have a planet, where is it. What are the coordinates? I'll punch them in right now and before you know it, we'll be back on your home turf. Then we can speak with your leader, and formulate a plan. If you're serious about this, then show me how serious you are. Trust us. You have every reason to. We aren't the ones targeting you. You're the ones that were targeting us."

"Of course we are targeting you. We knew that after the way that Pilgrim Tech treated you that you would be easy to manipulate to our will. We also knew that Pilgrim Tech wouldn't expect any blowback from you or your crew members after they paid you a million credits each. We were planning on using that money that each of you got to help fund our mission. But then something strange happened. We got somebody else. Somebody else on the inside. And then we came to a crossroads. A dilemma if you will. Now that we had somebody else, did we really need you? But our leader Commander Korr insisted that you were still a priority on this mission. That you were still the key, even though our original plan only consisted of one person on the inside. But now there are five in total, including the four of you. And things could get messy. So you can understand my trepidation in revealing the entirety of our mission statement."

I stood up, extending my hand, and gestured at the prisoner. At first, he didn't know what to do. He didn't know if this was a trap. If I was suckering him in. But after a few seconds of fearful silence, he shook my hand - all the while, I stared directly into his eyes.

I was trying to gain his trust. I was trying to make him see that I wasn't one of them – a member of Pilgrim Tech. And as I stared into his eyes, shaking his hand, I could see his front slowly eroding, like ice melting and turning into water.

The proverbial ice had been broken. We were now on an even playing field. We knew to what extent our loyalties lay and where they lay. He now knew my feelings toward the masters of Pilgrim Tech. But that didn't mean that I agreed with everything that he said. But obviously, I would be keeping that little gem to myself.

"So what do you say, now will you give me this coordinates?" I said, letting go of the prisoner's hand, but still staring directly into his eyes, trying to gain his trust.

The prisoner made a slight face, and I could tell that he was still not a hundred percent convinced – which was ironic, because I was in the same boat.

"Before I can give you the coordinates to our planet, you will need to speak to my Commander. I've been instructed to video call him once we came to some sort of agreement. So that is what we will do. I will give you the server address, and you will hail him. He will answer, and then you can ask him all the questions you want. After that, he will ask you all the questions that he wants. And hopefully, when the conference call is over, the two of you will be in agreement. And only then will you get the coordinates to our planet. He will be the one that gives them to you. I actually don't know them. I'm just a soldier. And if things don't go to plan, and you don't end up agreeing on the mission or its objective, then I guess I'm a dead soldier. Because there is no way I am getting home if that indeed is the case," the prisoner said.

I nodded, and smiled.

"Okay then, sorted. Give me the server address, and let's get this thing rolling."

The prisoner nodded his head, and reached into his pocket. We'd already searched him for weapons when we apprehended him earlier. So I knew that he wasn't armed, and I also knew that we were not in danger.

But he did pull out a piece of paper. It was scrunched up, and when I'd saw it earlier, I hadn't paid much attention to it. But now that it was in his hands, it all started to make sense. His story was starting to bind together quite nicely. If the server address truly did divert to a video call with his leader, then my trust in him would increase tenfold. But that didn't mean that he was my friend, nor did it mean that I was part of the Annex Rebel Fleet.

All it meant was that I was curious.

Curious to see how deep this rabbit hole goes.

***

Operational leader Sam was sweating profusely. He had spent the last ten minutes staring at himself in the bathroom mirror. The shared co-worker toilets were clean and sterile. But he couldn't help but feel dirty inside. He felt filthy. Filthy to be part of something so putrid that he could smell it from within the confines of the room he was in. A room that was tiled with white tiles, tiles that allowed the reflection of his face to beam back at him.

Along with the reflection in the mirror, operational leader Sam knew that he didn't look his best.

He looked a wreck. His hair was messy, and his shirt had sweat patches under his arms. He decided that it would be best to drench his face in cold water. Maybe that would cool down the fire that was raging within his head. He splashed handful after handful of water on his face, each time staring at his reflection as droplets dripped off his jawline and pattered into the porcelain sink. Each patter of water sounded like an earthquake in his head. His ears were muffled yet he could hear everything so clearly.

The chatter in the office on the other side of the door. The watercooler being used. The gulp inside the large bottle that hydrated everybody within the office block. The sound of people rustling papers. Shoes pressing into the carpet as people walked. The ticking of the clock on the wall. The buzz of the computer terminals. The beeping of the servers. The static in his head. And after drenching his face once again in the cool liquid running from the bathroom tap, he dried his face and convinced himself that he felt better.

Not wanting to waste any more time, he left the bathroom and entered back into the chaotic fray of the office. Even though Sam was the leader and the boss of this junket of Pilgrim Tech, word had gotten around that he had been summoned to the top. And after coming back downstairs and rejoining his team, he got the sense that they thought he was on his way out. Maybe he'd end up losing their respect, and if that happened, the very idea of completing his task would be even more difficult.

He was trying not to think about the consequences of failure right now. Pilgrim Tech had made their demands clear, and at the same time they had also made the repercussions clear to him. The Agent that he had spoken to had reassured him that failure was not an option. And it definitely wasn't on the cards anymore, not that it had ever been on the cards anyway. Sam took his job very seriously. But he had to take it even more seriously now that there was so much on the line.

So he couldn't wallow in his own self-pity any longer. And now that he felt fresh-faced, he was ready to tackle the task at hand. Like a lightning bolt from the sky above, he quickly made his way down the office toward the front. At the front, lay his desk. His desk faced the others. He'd opted not to have his own office, just to seem more approachable to his colleagues. Right at that moment, he felt a certain regret for that decision. Especially the way he was feeling. He wanted nothing more but to lock himself in a room, and hide away. But he couldn't do that. So instead of sitting at his desk, staring at his computer, he decided to make his way toward Maddie's booth.

Once he reached the booth, which was adjoined to the other booths in the office, he noticed how hard Maddie was working. She didn't even notice him standing next to her, observing her work. A few of her neighbors did though. They gave Sam a collection of uncertain looks. Looks that Sam couldn't differentiate between. He didn't know whether they were looks of pity, or looks of nervousness. Like he was a pariah of some sorts. Like being next to him was contagious, and anybody that associated with him would be summoned to the top as well.

But Sam ignored those looks, and leaned in closer to get a better look at Maddie's screen. She was still so engrossed in her work that she didn't even feel his breath on the back of her neck. She was staring at a satellite image of the Milky Way Galaxy, zoomed in at 25%. On that map, she was tracking certain ships. From the color legend below the schematic, operational leader Sam could see that some of those ships belonged to Earth, while others belonged to other alien nations.

Traffic in the Milky Way Galaxy was a little sparse today, probably on account of the attempted invasion of Earth. News had gotten around already, and the other nations within the Galactic Empire were nervous. The stock exchange mirrored that nervousness, the credit system taking a hit by a few thousand points. But operational leader Sam didn't give a crap about that sort of thing. The only thing that he gave a crap about was trying to figure out what the hell was going on.

"Track any of those Annex Rebel Fleet ships yet?" Sam said, startling Maddie as she turned around suddenly.

"Didn't see you there, sir. That's exactly what I've been doing, but unfortunately these guys are good. The only ships I've been picking up on this map are the ships that are currently looking for them.

Nothing else really. Apart from a few Sunday drive ships, going about their business, whatever business that may be," Maddie said.

She then turned back around toward her screen and started scrolling again.

There was a moment or two of silence as Sam was engrossed in the images that stared back at him. He was trying to work out a pattern - a possible pattern of stealth that the Annex Rebel Fleet were using to cover their tracks. They were hiding very well indeed. Pilgrim Tech had sent a few Snake Pit Fighters to track them down, but unfortunately, they'd returned unsuccessful. It was as if the rebels had vanished into thin air. Plus, even though they were using Earth sanctioned ships, they'd been smart enough to disable Pilgrim Tech issued trackers. These trackers were installed on every single ship that left Earth. It was meant to allow government officials to keep an eye on their population, surveying certain patterns that may help them understand the way people traveled and where they travel to.

Those trackers also came in handy as a way to advertise to certain demographics. If local earthlings traveled to alien planets using their personal space vehicle, Pilgrim Tech could sell demographical information to competing planets. But this wasn't no holiday board, and they weren't dealing with commercial spaceships here. They were dealing with stealth fighters that knew how to game the system, and how to use it to their advantage.

If they continued to remain off the radar, then there could be a serious threat to Earth's security in the coming hours. It meant that they could come and go as they pleased, without even setting off any automatic alarms. The manpower that would be needed to protect planet Earth from every possible angle would nearly bankrupt the Treasury, and cause a mass meltdown for the economy. Maybe these rebels were smarter than they looked. Maybe this was all part of their plan - a plan that if executed properly could very well work.

Operational leader Sam was starting to gain a little respect for these fighters. They had fought off everything, and so far, Pilgrim Tech were far behind the curve. They were playing catch up, but operational leader Sam knew that once they did catch up, the race was over.

"Zoom out a minute," Sam said, leaning in even closer, he was now able to smell Maddie's perfume.

She did as he said, and zoomed out to zero. What played back on the screen was a live panoramic view of the Galaxy. On the screen, hundreds of thousands of tiny blue dots moved at various speeds. If Maddie clicked on one of those dots, more information regarding that blue blip would pop up on the screen. The dots were ships. Red dots signified otherworldly ships, ships that weren't in control of Earth and blue dots signified ships that were owned by Pilgrim Tech and planet Earth. As one might expect, most of the blue ships were concentrated around planet Earth on the map. Unlike a ripple effect, the further away from Earth they scanned, the fewer ships there were. But one ship had caught operational leader Sam's interest. It was the furthest ship out, nowhere near any neighboring ships. And for that reason, Sam was curious to know more.

"What about that ship over there? Top left corner, near a cluster of red ships?" Sam said.

Maddie scrolled toward the cluster, and clicked on it.

"He's a bit far out. Judging by his trajectory, he's attempting to get as far away from Earth as possible. Maybe the news of the attempted invasion ruffled his feathers," Maddie said, reading up on the ship that she'd selected.

Operational leader Sam got even closer toward the screen, and did the same.

"The *Alpha Ship One*," Sam said, a little sarcasm present in his voice. "VIP status, I see," Sam continued, noticing that the ship had a strangely high priority setting on its record.

Judging by its size, and its age, one wouldn't come to the conclusion that the Alpha Ship One was of any importance. But according to its data log, and its registration documents appearing on the screen, the Alpha Ship One was very important. It was more important than the majority of the ships that he'd seen on the map already.

Most of the other ships were just bog standard commercial ships or army ships. Militarily and haulage ships were more or less the same. Both had the capability of defending themselves. Both had weapons on board, and both had free reign to pass through various nearby galaxies.

But VIP status ships were different. Even though a VIP could be tracked, tracking one needed a court ordered warrant. A warrant that would usually take a couple weeks to obtain. The thing with VIP status ships was that they usually could do what they want and go where they want, and not be disturbed.

But for some reason, this particular ship interested Sam. And the fact that it was a VIP ship interested him even more. But that wasn't what was peaking this curiosity, it was the fact that the ship looked as if it was getting out of dodge as fast as it could. And if it was truly leaving the Milky Way Galaxy, where was it going and was it for business or pleasure?

"Track that ship. Something seems a little off about it. Most VIP ships have been summoned back to Earth, in case the rebels attempt to kidnap any of the members on board. But this ship is ignoring all protocol. Something tells me that if we track it, we might learn a thing or two," Sam said, resting his hand gently on Maddie's shoulder.

She clicked on the ship a few times, and pressed on a tracking digital button, making Sam's order official. She then swiveled in her chair, and turned to her boss.

"Done and done," she said, smiling up at him. Sam couldn't muster a smile in return. There was nothing to smile about. He didn't have the time or patience to smile, he had a job to do. And that job was about to get a lot more interesting.

If things went his way, Pilgrim Tech would be catching up with the rebels soon. And when the Snake Pit Fighters and the Annex Rebel Fleet met for the second time, operational leader Sam hoped for his family's sake that they would end this before Pilgrim Tech ended them.

He wasn't taking their threat against his family lightly. As they had warned him, the sins of the father must be paid in full. He just hoped that the only people to pay for their supposed sins would be the rebels.

***

I stared at the screen expectantly. Now that I had been given the server address for the Annex Rebel Fleet Commander, I was waiting patiently as a connection attempt was made.

The ship's computer moaned and groaned as the old hard drives span at thousand rpm. Just like the ship itself, the computers onboard it were ancient by this day and age's standards. Pilgrim Tech had never seen the Alpha Ship One as a flagship vessel. They had seen it and its crew – including me – as fodder. And I had no qualms about that. In fact, I was happy to be part of a so-called subpar fleet.

Galactic fame and recognition had never interested me. The things that had interested me were out of my grasp anyway. Deep down, from the very first day I'd received my wings, I had always wanted to make a difference in this Universe. But unfortunately I knew my limitations and so did the bosses that governed me. I suppose the idea of getting contact with rebels that may share my same resentment toward the establishment was exciting. But I was still a little skeptical. After all, I was dealing with men that had attempted to kill me and my crew – no matter what they said, I knew that deep down within their black souls was nothing but evil.

The tell-tale signs were there. There had been many men before the so-called Annex Rebel Fleet that thought they were right, that they would just in their actions. But in my opinion, any man that chooses to make a point with bullets and knives is no better than the target of the point they are trying to make.

Men are all one in the same. They all share the same grievances, and the same faults. That means that in reality, there can be no good nor can there be any evil. But that doesn't mean that men don't try. There are men that try their very best to be righteous, only to fall at the last hurdle. And then there are men that hold no good within them, and choose to shun society and its keepers. Both types of men are part of the problem. And in my opinion, things won't change. At least not until men learn how to agree to disagree.

"I'm getting a strong signal on the other end boss," Philip said, manning the communications desk a few feet from me. He was sitting in his comms chair, overlooking the various signals coming inbound onto our computer system.

Looking at the big screen in front of me, I could tell that we were about to make contact with the Commander. The server address was correct. And whoever was on the other end of that server address had accepted our attempt at communication. After the screen had loaded, it went blank for no more than two seconds. I stared at the nothingness on the screen, my eyes focusing on every pixel, waiting for the undeniable moment of first contact with the Commander. And just as I expected, the blank screen disappeared and a new image popped up.

A stern face stared back at me. I saw a green light above my screen, indicating that face-to-face communication had been initiated. Both sound and visual playback was present. And the face staring back at me broke into an unexpected smile. A smile that showed a lack of oral hygiene, blackened teeth taking up a few inches of screen space. But it wasn't the man's teeth that I was interested in, it was what he had to say for his militia group and him choosing me and my crew as their so-called "key".

I didn't waste any time with pleasantries. Without even saying hello, or introducing myself, I went in for the kill.

"So – this is the face of the man responsible for destroying the space station that me and my crew were bunking at. I've met a few killers in my life, but none so ugly," I said, to the absolute dismay of the prisoner standing next to me.

I turned to see his face, it had gone completely white. He was about to say something when Dale appeared behind him and clocked him in the back of the head. The prisoner landed hard on the floor, out like a light.

The face staring back at me on the screen didn't look phased. In fact, he looked amused. This wasn't all just a show and dance for him. This was more than that. This was pent-up aggression. This was anger. And above all, this was revenge. I was fed up of being a pawn in other people's wars. I wasn't going to fall for the same thing twice. Pilgrim Tech may have used me before, but I wasn't going to allow these so-called freedom fighters to do the same.

"I can see that you are angry, and I understand your annoyance. But please allow me to explain myself and my cause," the Commander said, still smiling back at me, his teeth looking repulsive on the large screen in front of me.

But I wasn't interested in hearing his excuses. I had a lot to say, and not a lot of patience to listen to him whine on. I'd already heard what the prisoner had had to say, and although I agreed with some of his points, it was time for me to make a point of my own.

"You need to shut your mouth for a second. This isn't a negotiation. Your man already told me your mission statement, and quite frankly, I couldn't give a rat's ass what you and your militia of men want to accomplish. This isn't about you. This is about me, my crew and the Alpha Ship One. We have already been used more times than I care to remember. And I will not allow it to happen again. So, Commander, are you willing to shut your propaganda spewing mouth up for more than two minutes so I can tell you what I want out of this?"

The Commander's face soured a little. And even though he had been smiling seconds before, his smile had now disappeared into what I could only imagine to be total oblivion. He was a violent man. That much I could tell. He had never been spoken to like this before, and probably would never be spoken to like this again. I had been the first man to put him in his place in a very long time. He had the grand title of Commander, but to me he was nothing but a lout. And most likely, to him, I was nothing but an ant. A worker ant that he wanted to use for his misdeeds. But I wasn't willing to compromise on my crew or my ship. This wasn't going to be a hard sell. He wasn't going to persuade me into doing anything that I didn't want to do. And instead of acting like I was game for his jaunt against the Galactic Empire, I thought that it was best that I made things clear from the get go.

"I'll listen to what you have to say," the Commander said, clearing his throat a few times, and then taking a sip from a glass of water.

He was sitting in his captain's chair on his ship. I could see faces behind him, faces belonging to his crewmates, staring back at my reflection on their own big screen. They shared the same expression that the Commander shared. One of disbelief. It was obvious from their demeanor that they were rough and ready. They didn't usually have the time of day for people like me, but seeing that I had something they wanted, they would have to listen.

So I wasn't worried about pushing my weight around a little. This was a game of respect. And if these guys didn't respect me, then I could guarantee that my ship and my crew wouldn't be getting out of this one intact.

"You're damn right you're going to listen to me, I'm all you have. From what I've heard from your man on my ship, we are the key to your plan. But not every key opens every door. And I want you to know that, Commander. I don't want you to have any false hope when it comes to the Alpha Ship One. I don't want you to think that we are weak, and will easily bend to your will. I have met men like you before, and quite frankly, you don't scare me. I have two options; I can work with you and your men to help bring a new dawn to our planet and the Galactic Empire, or I can turn my ship back around and below your whole mission to kingdom come," I said, sitting back in my chair, the sound of the leather stretching as my bodyweight relaxed into the fabric.

Dale was still standing next to me. At his feet, the prisoner didn't move. And even if he did attempt to move, I'm sure Dale would put him back down where he belonged. We were running things. This was our ship. And we wouldn't allow these militiamen to frighten us out of orbit.

"I doubt that you understand what you are insinuating, Capt. Flynn. You talk as if you have some dirt on us, as if you know how to bring us down, down to your level, on an even playing field. But you are forgetting something. We outnumber you, and we sure as hell outnumber Earth's immediate defenses. I don't know what our man has told you, but I do know that he is only privy to a fraction of the information at play here. So before you start pounding your chest like an ape, trying to assert your dominance, just remember who the hell you are talking to," the Commander said, grinding his rotten teeth slightly as he spoke.

I smiled at the Commander. His threats weren't even registering with me.

"I feel as if I'm not making myself clear, Commander. Truth be told, I do not harbor any ill will toward your men or your mission. Your man made a good point when he tried to sell me on the idea of joining your militia. He made the point that Pilgrim Tech were corrupt and needed to be stopped. I didn't need him to tell me that. Me and my crew have seen it first-hand. We have experienced their corruption. And I am pretty sure that you are aware of the circumstances in which we experienced that corruption. But I'm not here to sell you on myself or my crew. And I hope to God that you are not here to do the same. I have heard enough about your militia. And I am certain that you have heard enough about us. The only question that truly remains is if we will join your crew, and help take down Pilgrim Tech."

The Commander was staring back at me, his face large on the equally large screen. He stopped gritting his teeth. He then broke out into a smile.

"I see. A man that wants to get straight to the heart of the matter. I respect that. And I understand what you are insinuating. You want me to know that you are fully capable of defending yourself, and you will not be persuaded into doing anything you do not wish to do. And while I appreciate the sentiment, please note that this is not how I do business. This isn't a dictatorship. Every man and woman that fights for the Annex Rebel Fleet has their reasons. I do not lord myself over my men or women. And even calling them my men and women pains me. Because this isn't what we are. We are not who we fight against. We are a group of like-minded individuals that want to bring a new dawn to mankind. So don't you worry yourself with the idea that once this is all said and done the Annex Rebel Fleet will just chew you up and spit you out. We are not Pilgrim Tech. We have a plan. And that plan is to eradicate the idea that men are disposable. *Expendable.* Because that is not what men are. We are much more than that. We are **expandable**. And we plan on expanding our presence in the Universe. But not via violent means, but via peace."

I stood up, nodded my head, and turned to Dale.

"You think he has a point? You think this will work?" I said, surprising both the Commander and Dale. But Dale didn't stutter.

"I suppose it's worth a try boss," Dale said, standing over the unconscious prisoner on the floor. I turned my head and faced the screen once again. The Commander looked confused. I intended to clear up that confusion.

"So there you have it Commander. The Alpha Ship One is officially in service. But just so you know, we don't work for you. We don't work for anybody. And even though you have your reasons for fighting the establishment, we have ours. And as far as I am concerned, our reasons are the only ones that matter. So don't go thinking that we are loyal to you. We are not. We are just loyal to making Pilgrim Tech pay for what they did to me and my crew. And once this is all over, you can go your separate way and we will go ours. You do as you please with the power you win from defeating

Earth. And we will do what we place with what we have left. I have no dreams of being a member of a new government. The only thing that I want to do is secure a future that is financially stable for my men and women. And maybe along the way, change the world for the better. But we'll see," I said.

The Commander nodded. His previous facial expression softened a little. Now that we were both on the same page and we had both laid out our true intentions, the reluctant relationship could begin.

"Good. It is done then. I don't expect you to kill or maim for my cause. I only have one mission for you and your crew. It's a simple mission. But it will change the dynamic of our Galaxy forever. A dynamic that is in desperate need of a shift. And a shift in momentum is what it will get. We are about to shake things up dramatically. Earth will not know what to do. But the people will. And that is all that matters."

I stared at the Commander, waiting expectantly for whatever order he was about to give.

"What is our mission then?" I asked, sitting back down in my seat.

"Kidnap the president of Pilgrim Tech, bring him to our planet, and make him confess to his crimes," the Commander snarled.

***

The non-descript man was sitting in his office. It was a small office, one shared by other low-key workers. The office was empty, most of the men and women that usually filled it were either on break or had gone home. The large space battle that had happened between the Annex Rebel Fleet and Earth's Snake Pit Fighter fleet had taken its toll on the workers at Pilgrim Tech. Some of them had been in the office for over thirty-eight hours. So the suits on the top floor had ordered some of the less important members of Pilgrim Tech to go home and catch some shuteye.

They'd also told him to go home, but he wasn't one to listen to authority, anyhow. He convinced them that he was better off working, making sure that any potential threats that could make themselves known would be dealt with as quickly as possible. And even though he was a low-key worker just like the rest of his office, he held some close ties with some of the members on the top floor.

They saw him as a valuable asset. But he wasn't an asset that they were willing to reward with a pay rise and a new position on a higher floor though. And deep down, the non-descript man knew that the fact that they used him so blatantly was one of the reasons why he was willing to risk it all to bring them down. But his unrewarded perks was one of the main reasons that he was even able to contemplate such a move. If they didn't see him as valuable, then he would not be able to be a successful operative for the Annex Rebel Fleet.

His position and his job played a major role in this operation. So a part of him was happy that Pilgrim Tech saw him like they did. If he had been able to get promoted, then maybe he would have been just like the rest of them, willing to turn a blind eye to corruption just to make a quick buck. The non-descript man was not like that. He held certain beliefs, beliefs that he was willing to throw caution to the wind for.

Sitting there at his desk, he stared at his computer screen. On the screen there was one solitary program opened up. It was in *windowed mode*, and he was staring blankly at the cursor as it flashed on and off. He was waiting for something. And going by the time on the bottom right corner of the screen, he wouldn't have to wait for much longer.

"Tick-tock," the nondescript man said under his breath.

The office was still empty around him. The only audible sound was coming from the ticking clock on his desk. He stared at that clock, and then at the screen, and then back at the clock, and then once more at the screen.

The cursor on the screen wasn't flashing anymore. It was typing. He watched as a message appeared on the chat box. Once the last letter was written, his heart began to flutter in his chest. He couldn't quite believe it. It was happening. They had done it. The plan was in motion. And there was no way they could stop it.

The mission is a go. Ship inbound. Awaiting distraction. ETA one hour.

The non-descript man grinned and then stood up. He clicked the '**X**' on the open chat window and then proceeded to shut his computer down. He didn't have much time to prepare the final touches for this monumental occasion. But he wasn't worried. He knew that an hour was plenty enough time to change the world… forever.

Chapter Nine

Operational leader Sam was gritting his teeth as he stared at his computer terminal. His nerves were beginning to get the better of him. Watching the screen, he wondered how significant the Alpha Ship One was. He had decided to put a tracker on the ship, observing its route and marking its projected course. But Sam was flabbergasted when he saw the ship turning a hundred-and-eighty-degrees, and making its way back toward Earth.

At first, Sam didn't think much of it. Maybe the ship had finally heard about the ruckus that had occurred at Sector Eight. But then Sam's intuition had pestered him into checking the ship's flight logs. Every ship that contained a tracker onboard was also an open book when it came to checking previous flights. All Sam had to do was turn back a slider on the program and observe the ship's previous flight paths and rest locations.

What surprised the operational leader the most was the fact that the ship had actually emanated from Sector Eight. And the timestamp on the ship log confirmed that the ship had vacated the area as soon as the trouble had commenced. So it didn't make much sense to Sam that the ship was meandering its way back toward the planet. Unless, of course, it was just flying past it. Neither the former or the latter could be proven until the ship reached Earth. But Sam was determined to make sure that he kept a watchful eye on the mysterious Alpha Ship One.

"Is the ship turning around?" Maddie asked.

She was standing behind Sam, much like he had been standing behind her half an hour previously. Sam swiveled in his chair and faced her.

"It looks that way. There's something off about that ship. I can feel it in my gut. Something is going on," Sam said, swiveling back in his chair and facing his computer terminal.

Sam battered the keyboard with his fingertips for a few minutes. Maddie watched on as he searched the archives of the mysterious Alpha Ship One. A strange thing was occurring though. Every time he searched for the ship and its previous mission logs, an access denied message appeared on the screen.

Sam was one of the most high-ranking members of the Pilgrim Tech, at least in the office currently, and should have been able to access every single log from every single ship that formed a cohesive part of Earth's fleet, be it commercial or otherwise. But the computer wasn't allowing him access to Alpha Ship One's records. And that just made Sam's suspicions stronger.

"What do you think the deal is with this ship?" Sam said, turning back to face Maddie who was deep in thought.

She looked at him, surprised by his question. He wasn't usually one to ask her advice, especially since she was just an office worker, and didn't hold much clout when it came to a position on the all elusive corporate ladder.

"Well sir, I definitely think something strange is going on here. Maybe you should ask the bosses on the top floor why the Alpha Ship One has VIP access?" She said.

Sam shrugged her shoulders.

"I guess you're right. Maybe I should ask. But judging by the mood on the top floor, I don't think it will get me anywhere of any use. They are already trying to find a scapegoat for this whole mess, and I don't want it to be me. So I guess I'm just going to keep my mouth shut, and get on with the job."

Maddie nodded her head. She thought that Sam was right, and was smart enough to know when to ask the difficult questions and when to keep quiet. But obviously, if the Alpha Ship One was playing an active part in the rebels attacking Earth, Pilgrim Tech would be just as sour on Sam if they found out that he had been tracking the ship and had just ignored the potential warning signs.

But Sam wasn't stupid, and she knew that he had a plan, even if he wasn't divulging it to her. She trusted him implicitly, and if that meant her falling on his sword, and defending his job, she would do just that. But hopefully, it wouldn't come to that.

"What the heck?" Sam said, sitting up in his seat, surprised at what he saw on his screen.

The Alpha Ship One was still making its way toward Earth, and would be about an hour away until it reached his jurisdiction. But that wasn't what was surprising Sam. The ship's radar had come online, and was now pinging Earth. It was as if the Alpha Ship One was trying to contact Earth. Pinging wasn't part of most spaceships protocols. If contact had to be made with Earth, it would usually be over radio or video call. But the Alpha Ship One was using an old form of communication. A form of communication that was hard to detect. And also just as hard to decipher. It was similar to Morse code. And Sam was eager to know what the pinging translated to.

"You need to get somebody from communications down here. We have a situation," Sam said, staring intently at the screen, listening to the radio waves ping off his ears.

He was right – this was definitely a situation in need of a trained comms guy, but he wasn't sure if it was a situation he wanted any part of. But he had no choice in the matter. This was happening whether he liked it or not. But at least now there was some light at the end of the tunnel. A bright light in the form of a radio transmission.

The Alpha Ship One was now without a doubt a ship of interest.

***

I was feeling rather jangly. I couldn't even hold my hands over the controls without them shaking uncontrollably like an alcoholic missing his fix of hard liquor. Now that I had been briefed by Commander Korr on the part that the Alpha Ship One would play in this mission, I felt a little relieved. But that didn't stop me feeling like the whole Universe was weighing down on me, crushing my shoulders. This whole thing was a big deal. There were no second chances with this, it was either revolution or revolt. And to most, they represent the same thing. Unorganized chaos, coupled with violence. Overthrowing a government would not be easy, and I knew there would be a lot of turmoil after this. But I believed that we were doing the right thing.

I don't regret much in my life, but I do regret not asking for a general consensus from my own crew. They were putting their lives on the line unequivocally for something that I had decided we'd be part of. I just hoped that they felt the same way as me. I just hoped that they would understand where I was coming from, and where I wanted us to be heading to. But now it was too late to ask them for their opinion. They were in this whether they liked it or not.

I had a feeling that one or two of them did not like it.

Philip hadn't said a word since. He was sitting at his comms desk, observing lines of communication within the Milky Way Galaxy. So far, according to him at least, nobody had attempted to contact us.

So that meant that we weren't being suspected of anything. I was willing to bet that the guys at Pilgrim Tech were scouring the Galaxy for suspicious looking ships. I knew that the Annex Rebel Fleet was serious about this endeavor, and had observed through my own readings that their ships were not trackable. But the problem was that the Alpha Ship One was trackable. And there was no way that I could disable the tracker onboard. It was pre-installed, and wasn't over-rideable. We were stuck. Stuck in plain sight. And anybody that didn't take a liking to my ship, or saw it as suspicious, would be able to follow it on radar.

So that meant that I would have to be cautious when exiting warp drive and entering Earth's atmosphere. I'd need to be just like any other ship, going about its business, not attracting suspicion. If I managed that, then I knew that this mission of ours would go off without a hitch. But then again, kidnapping the president of Pilgrim Tech and taking him back to the rebel's planet was bound to be a little bumpy. I expected things to get serious, and get serious fast.

I just didn't know how serious things would become.

If I had known, then maybe I would have done things a little differently. But hindsight is great and all, but the reality of the matter was things were far from done, and wouldn't be done until a good while from now. So I had to remain calm, and pilot my ship and my crew to a revolution. A revolution that I believed in, and hoped to God that my crew believed in as well.

"I hope you're happy with yourself, Capt. Flynn," Philip said from his seat, his hands over his comms unit, fiddling with a few dials.

I looked up at him, and tried to form a smile. But smiling was hard. Especially when I realized that Philip did not share the same excitement about our mission. I guess my trepidation in not asking the crew their opinion on the rebels or the rebels' cause was correct. And maybe it would have proven a lot easier to have had a vote on our participation, but then again, I was the Captain, and I chose our missions, not them.

"I'm as happy as a man can be, considering the situation that we are in. I did what I had to do, Philip. I hope that you can understand that. I hope that you can understand that this is the perfect time to affect change back on Earth, a change that will make sure that we as a group, as a crew, can survive the turbulent times ahead. That's all I can hope for. And if things don't go our way, I'll hold my hands up high, and take the blame," I said, trying to smile at Philip, trying to regain his trust.

But I could see that my efforts were futile. He wasn't interested in hearing what I had to say. And if I wasn't careful, I suspected that he could turn Teresa against me. Especially since two of them had a lot of history together. They had come onboard the Alpha Ship One together, also prisoners on the Ursine planet, and played a big part in destroying that planet.

"I don't want you to take the blame for this, Capt. Flynn. All I want you to do is reassure me that this is the right thing to do. I mean, look at who we are associating with. Two bads don't make a right. And two forces of evil certainly don't make a revolution. This isn't about toppling a corrupt government, nor is it about fighting for a noble cause. This is about deciding our future, and the future of our children. And I just want to know if our children can prosper under a new government. A government brought on by a revolution - a revolution incited by rebels. Or are they doing just fine right now?"

I sat there for a few seconds, staring at Philip, and then at Teresa, who was standing next to him. She didn't look like she was excited about the prospect of our mission. I guess I understood why, seeing that we were not gaining anything from this apart from uncertainty.

Then again, we were a mercenary ship. We always have been. And we will always be a mercenary ship. But money tends to smooth the hard edges of uncertainty. And there was certainly no money in this, just hard edges, edges that pricked, edges that surrounded us and our future. But sometimes things were worth fighting for that didn't involve financial gain. Sometimes it made sense to put everything on the line.

"I don't have all the answers Philip. I don't know what will happen after this, but I do know we have to work as a team. We cannot fall out over this. We have to remain united. That being said, I don't want you to forget who's in charge here. I am. And this is my ship. You work for me. You all work for me. And I have chosen to accept a mission that could benefit us tenfold in the future. We could finally be part of a society that doesn't need a mercenary ship. We could be part of a society that openly trades with otherworldly aliens, bringing planets together and keeping humans prosperous."

Philip nodded his head, and stood up.

"Yes, it's true, we do need to remain a team. Whatever you choose, I'll stand by your side. You saved my life back on the Ursine planet. And if that means I have to save your life in the future, so be it. I'm going for a piss," Philip said, walking toward the double doors, and leaving the bridge. The doors automatically closed behind him, making a whoosh sound, rattling against my ears.

Nothing but silence followed his exit. A silence that was crushing and suffocating. I needed to get my thoughts together. And truth be told, I thought that a stiff drink was in order.

"Anybody fancy a refreshment?" I said, to no reply.

Not wanting to risk looking like more of a loser, I stood up and also made by way toward the double doors. If nobody wanted to drink with me, that was just fine. I was more than happy to drink for the lot of them. I had an hour to unwind before reaching Earth and its armies. And as things were, I thought a little Dutch courage was just what the doctor had ordered.

***

Commander Korr was feeling the strain. The pressure was starting to mount. It was starting to get to him. And he feared deep down that it was starting to become a little too much for him. But he was made of strong stuff. Stuff that his father had encroached on him. He was not the sort of man to back down from a challenge. And this was definitely a challenge. One of the biggest challenges that he had ever faced in his life. He was less than an hour away from realizing his dream. From inciting a revolution. A revolution that the people of Earth would be talking about for centuries to come.

They would teach his revolution in schools. Much like they taught the history of Rome, and other ancient civilizations. Civilizations that rose to the top of their age, and conquered everything in sight. But for Commander Korr, this wasn't about conquering other planets.

This was about putting an end to the treachery that the government had forced upon its people. He had seen his father suffer at the hands of the government. When they didn't have any use for him anymore, they threw his father away like trash. And not thinking twice, they hired another schmuck in his place.

That was how things worked back on Earth. It was an assembly line of manpower. Manpower that had very little rights. But the people of Earth had become used to their abusers. Become used to the idea that some people achieve and others flounder. But Commander Korr knew that was nonsense. Commander Korr knew that people had the power to effect change. And he also knew that change was very much in order. People had been crying out for it for the past couple hundred years. And the government pretended to listen, but they did nothing in response.

Nothing of any significance anyway. Sure, they pretended to invite change in the form of democracy. But it was all a thin veil, a veil that Korr and the people that he now commanded could see through. It was men and women like his that were the new warriors of change. And he had faith in them that they would succeed in their mission to overthrow the putrid government that lorded over them.

The Commander knew that this would be a battle best fought in ignorance. He knew that he had to be ignorant to the fact that the government outnumbered and outgunned his men. He knew that he had to be ignorant to the fact that if he was caught rebelling against the establishment, then every person that he knew, and every person that his crew knew, would suffer. But ignorance was bliss, and Commander Korr was feeling blissful. To him, the danger of being defeated was worth the idea of effecting permanent change on his planet.

"Okay, this is it," Commander Korr said, holding a microphone to his mouth, speaking to his pilots stationed on his rebel planet, ready to fly into action.

"This is the moment we affect the history books. This is the moment we take down a government that oppresses other alien species in our Galaxy and galaxies far beyond. This is the moment we open up a new line of communication between other planets. This is the moment we take our own future into our own hands, just like our forefathers did hundreds of years ago. Sometimes change is needed. Sometimes that change is long overdue. And other times it is just an idea. But we know that this change, the change we are about to effect, is real. But make no mistake about it, it started as an idea. An idea that every single one of you helped shape. And now that it is fully formed, we can advance our mission.

"I have tasked each and every single one of you to be a part of the spearhead arrow that will strike itself into the heart of corruption. It is with this arrow that we will wage our war. And every war starts with a bang. It is this bang that will help us get to our target. Once we get that target, the President of Pilgrim Tech, we will've become victorious in our first battle. There will be many battles after this. But it is you, the formation of the arrow, the first arrow to penetrate the corrupt atmosphere around Earth, that will be recognized as the pioneers of this war.

"You are all game changers. And believe me, the game has changed. I just want you to know that your sacrifice on the battlefield will be forever recognized. And even though the humans outnumber you tremendously, know that once we have our target, we will outnumber them. Because all they will have left are numbers, while we will have the true substance of this battle. We will have the core. We will have the Earth. We will have the seas. We will have the mountains. We will have their leader. And once their leader becomes our prisoner, they too become ours. Ours to do as we please with. And it won't be long until they surrender their arms and accept their new leaders - us," Commander Korr said, putting the microphone back down and watching as his men got ready to fulfill their obligations.

The pilots within the ship's roar in approval. After a minute or so of jubilation, a quietness settles around the men and women on the rebel planet. Some of them watch as ship after ship ascends toward the skies. Before they know it, there are few ships left. The ships that had exited the atmosphere make their way toward their target. Earth doesn't know it yet, but a storm is heading their way.

A storm that promises to rip the fabric of society apart.

Chapter Ten

"Red alert, I repeat, red alert!" The voice on the tannoy system said, alerting everybody in the facility of the imminent danger that was approaching.

The non-descript man was working at his desk when the voice came over the sound system. It startled him into action. He had let time pass him by. He was supposed to have been keeping an eye on the clock, psyching himself up in preparation of his sole objective. But instead, he'd been reading up on some research, research based on previous revolutions.

But the time for preparing was now over, and the time to act was upon him. The voice on the tannoy was still repeating the same sentence over and over again. *Red alert. Red alert.* To the uninitiated, what was about to happen was indeed a red alert. But to him, and the rest of the rebels on the mysterious planet, this wasn't a time for fear, this was a time for joyous celebration. After years of planning, their vision of a revolution was about to become a fully-fledged picture.

Before the non-descript man left his office, he took a final look at his computer screen. On the right-hand side of the computer screen, right at the top, was a small digital picture frame. The picture frame stared back at him. It reminded him that he had a family. But it also reminded him that he was most likely not going to see them ever again.

But that was a price that he was willing to pay. And by God was he willing to pay it in full! But something had caught his eye on the left-hand side of the screen. A memo had come through. Its icon was flashing, trying to get his attention. He was torn on whether he should get a move on or whether he should read the memo.

He decided on the latter. He quickly opened the memo, surprised to see what the contents of it was. Pilgrim Tech had circulated an internal memo, a memo that had also been sent to him, and in that memo was a live feed of an approaching rebel fleet. The nondescript man wondered if Pilgrim Tech had meant to send the memo to him. He was just a lowly employee. He thought that maybe they would want to keep this sort of thing under wraps, as to not cause a panic. Not that he was panicking. He'd expected the rebel fleet. He welcomed them even. Because he knew that he wouldn't be able to accomplish his mission if the rebels weren't involved. He needed them to cause a distraction. A big enough distraction to put the fear of God in Pilgrim Tech.

And judging by the chaos outside, the sound of running footsteps and shouting voices, the fear of God was very much invoked right at that very minute. Satisfied with the contents of the memo, the nondescript man got to his feet, grabbed his briefcase, and ran toward the exit. Pushing the door open, he now found himself in a hallway. The hallway was bustling with activity, people running from left to right, looking like headless chickens. But he had his head firmly screwed onto his shoulders. He knew exactly where he was supposed to go.

Deciding to go right, he quickly walked down the hallway, barging past some of the frightened employees that surrounded him. Most of them weren't paying any attention to him. But he was paying attention to every single one of them. It was like he was walking in slow motion, his ears were muffled, and his heart was pounding in his chest. Every single person he passed, he drank their expression in.

He was savoring the moment. It was happening just like he'd imagined. The looks on their faces were priceless. He'd go as far as to say that he was enjoying it. Enjoying the chaos. Enjoying the fright. Enjoying the fear. But he didn't have time to enjoy it for much longer. Before he knew it, he was taking the elevator up toward the top floor.

And just like he'd planned, he was outside the bigwig's office block before he knew it. The trip in the elevator had passed without incident. And most of it was a blur. It was as if one minute he had blinked, and he was downstairs, and the next he was upstairs, staring at the grainy surface of the wooden door, about to knock on it. A wave of emotion crashed over him, some of it was self-doubt, whilst rest was self-pity.

Part of him didn't know if he could go through with this. While the other part of him wanted nothing but success. Failure was not an option. And he feared that he would fail if he didn't play his cards right. So he cleared his throat, closed his eyes, thought of his happy place, and then breathed. After exhaling, he opened his eyes, and knocked on the door three times.

Somebody summoned him in. He was now on the cusp of executing his plan. Years of research was about to culminate in this very moment. He reached into his jacket pocket, pulled out a gun, and walked into the room. Without thinking twice, he aimed the weapon, and fired. Five men were sitting around a table. Four of them now had bullet holes in their heads. One of them remained speechless, staring up at him, blood-soaked papers on the desk in, a look of wretched fear entrenched in his eyes.

"Sorry to bother you, Mr. President, but you're coming with me," the nondescript man said, realizing that for the first time in four years he was no longer operating in the shadows, but he was now the shadow, the shadow of darkness that was engulfing the corrupt offices of Pilgrim Tech.

Things were about to change forever. And he was the architect of that change. A change that was both inevitable and long overdue.

***

I put the ship into manual mode, taking control of the vessel as it disengaged from warp drive speeds. The view from the outside quickly changed from melded stars and black blotches in the atmosphere to a massive battle. We had reached Earth, and just above it, the so-called distraction was playing out. Thousands of Annex Rebel Fleet ships were battling Snake Pit Fighters. And we were about to get stuck right in the middle of it all. So a little evasive maneuvering was called for. I tilted and turned the controls to the right, banking the ship, and trying to duck under all of the action.

"Sweet Jesus, it's really kicking off down here!" Dale said, taking his position on the gunner's seat, scoping out the battlefield in front of us with his onboard weapon's reticle.

Teresa and Philip were sat down in their seats. They weren't doing much other than staring at the battle that was unfolding around us. The prisoner had been tied to a chair, and was dozing in and out of consciousness. I started to become a little worried about him, seeing that he had been out cold for at least an hour now, and I didn't really want him to die on us. Especially if we were supposed to be returning to the Annex Rebel Fleet's hideout. The last thing I wanted to do was antagonize them by presenting a dead soldier to the Commander.

His dead soldier. Not exactly the best way to start a working relationship, in my opinion.

But the prisoner's well-being would have to take a backseat while I ducked and dived my way through the treacherous battle that was taking place around us and Earth. I didn't have much time to analyze the particulars of the battle, but I could see that the Snake Pit Fighters were greatly outnumbered, and Earth would have to send even more reinforcements to defend the sovereignty of the planet.

The distraction was working rather well. Earth and its people would be so bamboozled by the attack, that all of their attention would be on the battle, and they hopefully wouldn't even see us approaching the planet. But I had something up my sleeve. I knew that the Alpha Ship One was decked with a cloaking device, and that would help us get past some of the approaching Snake Pit Fighters that were wanting to get in on the action around us. So I engaged the cloaking device, and flew under the radar.

"Won't they pick us up at flight control?" Philip asked when he noticed what I was doing.

It was a genuine question and was also a genuine concern of mine. He was the communications guy, so I was hoping he had the answer to that. But I decided to buff my way through the question, and answered him with a half-truth.

"Who knows? I'm hoping that the battle will distract them enough to let us slip by without much impediment. But then again, maybe the battle will just strengthen Earth's borders, and if we enter without the right authority, we'll be blown to smithereens. But every cloud has a silver lining, and if that is truly our fate, then we won't even feel it. So I guess we have that going for us," I said, still manually steering the ship, slowly but steadily approaching the blue planet, seconds from entering its atmosphere.

"Yeah, sounds like a solid plan to me," Teresa said.

The battle was still going on around us, and was beginning to get quite dense. There were a lot of ships involved in this skirmish, but I managed to get past without attracting any unwanted eyes on us. Obviously, the Annex Rebel Fleet knew our purpose on the battlefield. We were a Trojan horse. A Trojan horse that was supposed to penetrate Pilgrims Tech's defenses, and scuttle away with one of their men. But not just any man. Their President.

"You really think this is going to work Capt. Flynn? You actually think we are going to be able to kidnap the president of Pilgrim Tech, and take him back to the rebel stronghold? I mean we've been in some tough situations before, and I don't doubt your skill as a pilot, but I do doubt your intentions. I'm still struggling to understand how the hell this is going to help anybody? If the rebels do get a hold of the leader of Pilgrim Tech, then what chance do the people on Earth have fighting against a government that has nothing to lose?" Dale asked.

I was quite impressed with his vocabulary. He was a big brutish man, and I'd never heard him talk with such indignation before. But this wasn't the time to be impressed. And I guess his concerns were valid. But I didn't have the answers that he wanted. I had no idea why I was doing this. I guess I could liken it with a decision made in the heat of the moment. But the difference between a split-second decision that changes your life forever, versus this decision, was the fact that I'd been steeping in my own anger for a very long while. This wasn't just in the heat of the moment; this was anger that I had felt toward the establishment for so long, that it just felt normal to hate the men at the top. And I guess I felt as if this was my moment to prove that the little guy could win. That the little guy could change the world for the better. But I didn't have enough time to articulate that sentiment to Dale.

I had a ship to control. I had a Trojan horse to march on forward to victory. And we were ever so close to penetrating the atmosphere.

"ETA; five seconds," Philip said, monitoring the ship's vitals as we entered the outer crust.

The ship jolted up and down, side to side, and then began to rattle as we crashed into Earth's atmosphere. I steadied the ship somewhat, but the journey was still a little bumpy. I entered the exact coordinates of Pilgrim Tech's headquarters, and watched as the ship took a hard left, and zoomed towards its objective.

After a few seconds, the jolty ride stopped, and the clouds appeared. We were now back on Earth, and the skies were crystal blue above us. But at the speed we were going, it wouldn't take long to reach the continent. And on that continent, the continent that used to be known as North America, was the headquarters of Pilgrim Tech.

"Give me a rough estimate on arrival?" I asked, turning in my chair, facing Philip. He looked up at me and shrugged his shoulders.

"Computer's telling me two minutes. I guess we got lucky. If we'd hit Earth from the other side, then it would have been a few hours," Philip said.

I agreed with him. We'd been lucky so far. It was no secret that you could warp drive in space, but going such a speed on Earth was unwise. The skies above were chock-a-block full of spacecraft, and other air vehicles. Exceeding the speed of two-thousand miles an hour was not advisable. Unless of course you wanted to collide with a commercial jetliner.

I could see the continent approaching. North America was still such a beautiful piece of land. And even after many wars on that land, I still felt as if it was my home. It made me feel peaceful. It made me feel welcome. But after what I was about to do, I doubted that I'd ever see it again. I was, in effect, turning my back on my home. I was turning my back on my government. But it was for the greater good. It was to free the people of Earth. And I just hoped beyond hope that I could do just that.

"Thirty seconds," Philip said.

We were now roaring over the continent. A couple of seconds ago we had been over New York, and now we found ourselves over Minnesota. In about ten more seconds we would reach LA. And once we reached California, we'd dive toward the headquarters.

"Five seconds," Philip said, as I counted down in my head.

I started to slow the vessel down a little, while at the same time banking to the right. The golden coasts of California shone back up at me. I had taken one last look at the beauty below before I nosedived the aircraft toward its final destination.

The Alpha Ship One was an old ship, that much was true, but it was a trusted ship. It held VIP status. So any prying eyes would dismiss our presence as nothing more than routine. We didn't have to follow the rules. After what happened to us, after being marooned on the Ursine planet, and saving the world from certain annihilation, we were given special privileges.

It was with these privileges that I made the decision to divorce myself from the tyranny that I'd been subjected to. So as we approached the Pilgrim Tech headquarters, the automatic scanners let us through immediately.

Our VIP status had paid off. And now there was no turning back.

"There it is! Slowing down, forty percent power, turning off cloaking device. According to my map, the ship hangar is right in front of us, bearing down a few degrees," Philip said, watching his monitor like a hawk.

He was right. I could see the approaching landing lights. The hangar was nearby. Pilgrim Tech headquarters used a tunnel-like-hangar embedded into rock and granite as a landing strip. There were no runways on the surface, and we would need to maneuver the ship through a long dark passageway that burrowed through the earth to reach the security hangar where the Pilgrim Tech suits would most likely be waiting for a pickup.

From what I understood, this distraction would allow us to masquerade as an evacuation ship. The Annex Rebel Fleet had thought this out thoroughly. They had left no stone unturned. They knew what protocols were followed when an emergency occurred. And they knew that the only way they were going to get a hold of the Pilgrim Tech President was if they infiltrated the department from within. Apparently, they had someone on the inside, someone working to get the Pilgrim Tech president on board this ship. But that didn't mean that I still wasn't nervous. A lot could go wrong.

"Reducing power, sixty percent, thrusters activated," Philip said.

I slowed the Alpha Ship One down to a crawl. The runway lights were nearing. The onboard computer was warning me of a landing, whilst telling me to retract. I ignored the warnings, and lowered the ship a little more. I lined the vessel up with the landing lights, and propelled the ship toward the security gate blocking the tunnel.

As we approached, an automatic scan blinked in front of us, analyzing the credentials of the Alpha Ship One once again. After a few seconds, a light went green above the gate, and the gate opened automatically, allowing us to enter the tunnel.

"Lights on," Philip said.

The tunnel lit up, revealing a mile or so of runway in front of us. It was void of any activity. Usually, there were hundreds of ships landing and taking off. But the distraction above us, orbiting space, was doing its job. Most of the ships had left. And I didn't think they'd be returning in the meantime. So far, the Annex Rebel Fleet was winning. I didn't know if they'd win the battle, but they were certainly about to win the war if this went off without a hitch.

"Approaching the designated hangar. Landing gear activated. Power reduced by ninety percent. Thrusters deactivated. The runway is all yours, Capt. Flynn," Philip said as I rattled the controls slightly, trying to even out the ship.

The wheels touched the tarmac, and the engine brakes roared to life. The Alpha Ship One came to a stop at its predesignated area, right outside of the Executive Hangar. The door opened, and I made a right, taxiing slowly into the dark facility.

I saw two people standing on a platform, waiting for a pickup. That pickup was me. I only recognized one of them. Even though they both looked like ants from where I was sitting, the one I'd recognized was without a doubt the Pilgrim Tech President.

It was the same guy that had debriefed me and my crew once we'd returned to Earth after our bust-up with the Ursines. It was the exact same guy that had given me one million credits to keep my mouth shut.

Thankfully, it was the same guy that I was about to kidnap.

The ship came to a stop, and I opened the side doors, a small platform ejected out of the Alpha Ship One, and interlocked with the platform on the hangar. I quickly got off my seat, and made my way toward the door. To my surprise, the Pilgrim Tech president was already being pushed into the Alpha Ship One. I took a step back, a little terrified of his potential reaction. But then I remembered that I was in control. That I was the boss. That he no longer called the shots.

"Welcome on board the Alpha Ship One. I hope you have a pleasant journey," I said, grabbing the man in the suit by the scruff of the neck, and shoving him into a chair.

"I demand to know the meaning of this! Do you not know who I am?" The Pilgrim Tech President said as I tied him to his chair and put a gag in his mouth.

The son of a bitch didn't even recognize me. He was totally oblivious to who I was, or who my crew were. Not to mention he didn't even flinch when I told him that he was onboard the Alpha Ship One. But I guess I should've known better. He was a politician after all, and politicians only remember one thing; and that's the amount of money they have in their bank accounts.

"Although this little reunion is sweet and all, I would suggest that you get us off this planet as soon as you can. They'll be looking for him. And I'm pretty sure they'll be after us for what I did to his fellow Cabinet members," a voice said from behind me.

I turned around, and standing in front of me was another man in a suit. This man had blood on his lapel. And a gun in his hand. He was the man on the inside. That much I could tell. I didn't even have to ask for his name. There was no point anyway. He was right. We needed to get a move on. But before we could, I had one request.

"No weapons onboard the ship. Toss it out or you're not coming with us," I said.

The man stood there for a few seconds, visibly torn with the ultimatum I'd just given him. But he didn't voice his displeasure. He nodded his head slowly, disengaged the magazine from the gun, tossed the clip out, popped a bullet out of the chamber, threw the bullet out of the ship, and handed the gun to me.

"Bullets and magazines are replaceable. But that gun means something to me. So when we get to the Annex Rebel Fleet's planet, I hope I can count on you to reunite me with my most trusted weapon," the guy said.

I nodded my head, holstered the gun and quickly made my way toward the captain's seat. I sat down, retracted the platform back into the ship, closed the automatic doors, and taxied back toward the runway.

"It's a little chaotic up there, so I suggest you all buckle up, this is probably going to be a bumpy ride," I said, pushing the power throttle up toward a hundred percent.

The Alpha Ship One rattled once again as it flew down the runway tunnel. Seconds later, a bright light pounded against my eyes as we roared out of the tunnel and soared up into the sky.

We had a battle to get to. And once we got to it, we had to get past it. And I had a feeling that would be easier said than done. Especially now we had such precious cargo on board. Cargo that no doubt its owners would miss. But how far were they willing to go to get their cargo back?

I dreaded to think.

Chapter Eleven

The expert looks up at operational leader Sam and frowned. He was beyond confused. The expert had no clue what he was listening to. Sam had called him in for his opinion, and was hoping that he had some idea of what the pinging signal coming from the Alpha Ship One meant. But the man was just as baffled as he was.

"I don't know what you have here, it could take me a few days to even get to grips with this code. So I think you are going to have to be patient. That or we make a few educated guesses," the expert said.

He was sitting on a chair that had been pulled up to operational leader Sam's desk. Everybody else was working around them. The other office workers were far too consumed in their duties to even pay attention to the unfamiliar man. Normally, an outsider would be regarded with suspicion. But this man was safe from judgment today. The only judgment he would be receiving would be from operational leader Sam himself, who expected much more of him.

"Well, how about you make some educated guesses then? Couldn't hurt, could it?" Sam said.

He was torn between staring at his computer terminal in front of him, and catching a glimpse of Maddie as she worked at her desk. She wasn't staring back at him though. And in hindsight, finding out what the pinging meant mattered more than ogling a pretty girl.

"I'm a scientist Sam, and scientists don't make a habit of guessing. But, if you were to twist my arm, I guess I could materialize some theories," the expert said.

His eyebrows were bushy, and seemed to arch every time a syllable left his lips.

The two of them were staring at Sam's computer screen. For the past thirty minutes, they'd been examining the sound waves coming from the Alpha Ship One. The program they were using took up the whole of the computer screen, and since they had started analyzing the sound, neither of them had been paying any attention to the schematic map - the map that showed the current location of the Alpha Ship One.

If they had been paying attention, then maybe they wouldn't have been wasting time on getting to grips with the signal or the tracker. They would have been trying to stop the Alpha Ship One from doing what it was doing right NOW.

"Okay then, materialize some theories. Hit me with what you have Dr.," Sam said.

The expert nodded, cleared his throat and then tapped his fingers on the desk. He was tapping out a pattern, the same pattern that the signal contained. It was like a beat to the scientist's ear. A beat that he recognized. And just like Sam had originally thought, the beat – or signal, whatever you want to call it – was basically Morse code. What the scientist was doing as he patted his fingers on the hardwood desk was familiarizing himself with the pattern. And after a minute or two of uninterrupted fidgeting, the scientist looked up at Sam and smiled.

"Okay, if the signal/tracker has elements of Morse code within it like I think it does, then what you are hearing translates roughly to a phrase," the scientists said.

His eyebrows were still bushy, and they still arched as he spoke.

"Spit it out then, I haven't got all day Dr.! I don't know if you've realized, but we are in crisis. I'd like to keep an eye on the ship, and its current route, and I can't do that if we're splitting hairs here, now can I?" Sam said.

The scientist nodded his head gingerly, and tried to act as if he wasn't offended by Sam's request to get on with it. Although the man was being stubborn, and quite blunt, the scientist understood the urgency of the matter. And after tapping his fingers a few more times, he felt confident enough to lay down his theory.

"The phrase I am picking up off the signal is; *'follow the leader'*."

Sam scrunched his eyes suddenly, trying to get to grips with what that could possibly mean. His head swam with various ideas. Some of them made sense to him, while others were just nonsensical. The Alpha Ship One were not leading anything or anybody, as far as he knew, anyway. So what could it mean? Were they the leaders? Or were the Annex Rebel Fleet the so-called leaders? But then again, what if the Morse code theory was wrong? What if there was no leader to follow, and this was all just a waste of time?

Sam couldn't help but think that there were still many questions unanswered here. The fact that the expert himself had basically admitted to this whole thing being a theory, meant that he couldn't run with it. It also meant that finding out the true meaning of the tracker and its pinging signal would have to wait. Sam was still uncertain of many things, but one of them stuck out like a sore thumb to him.

"Why would they keep the tracker on? If they are working with the Annex Rebel Fleet or have any part in this Civil War that's about to erupt, then why the hell would they be trying to contact us? Surely they would want to remain under the radar?" Sam asked.

The expert raised his eyebrows again, and then shrugged his shoulders. He excelled loudly, and started tapping his fingers once again on the table.

"Maybe they want you to actually follow them? Maybe it's as simple as that?" The expert said.

Sam was about to retort to the man when a loud alarm sounded off in the office. It frightened him something rotten. He stood to attention, analyzing the ambiance of the room. His staff were running around like the ill-minded at an asylum breakout. Maddie was now next to him. She had a horrified look on her face. A look that he deciphered within a second. Something bad had happened. Something very bad indeed. His gut was telling him it was something to do with the Alpha Ship One. He quickly bent over his computer, and exited the full-screen program that he had been on for the past thirty odd minutes. And sure enough, his gut feeling rang true. Staring him dead in the face was the live schematic map that he'd been surveying on his computer.

The Alpha Ship One was no longer on the other side of the Milky Way Galaxy. It was now in its atmosphere – to be precise – the Alpha Ship One was flying over Los Angeles right at that very second!

"What the heck? When the hell did they get here?" Sam said, feeling mightily stupid for not intercepting whatever this new development was. He knew in his heart of hearts that the Alpha Ship One was the reason behind the alarm. He also knew that whatever bad news Maddie was about to lay out him, the Alpha Ship One was definitely the reason behind that as well.

His gut had never steered him wrong before.

"Sir, we have a major situation unfolding. The President of Pilgrim Tech has been kidnapped!" She said, her breathing was shallow and deep, making the words that she was speaking seem harsh and dry.

She was choking on her own saliva, and Sam knew exactly how she was feeling. He could hardly get his words out as well.

His mouth felt like it was being ravaged by sandpaper. A cold sweat was dripping down his back. His heart was beating out of control in his chest. His legs and knees felt weak. He had to sit down. And when he did sit down, he saw the computer screen staring back at him once again.

All of a sudden, a theory popped into his head. A theory of his own. What if the President of Pilgrim Tech was on the Alpha Ship One? What if the so-called leader that the Morse code spoke of was in fact their actual leader, the President? What if Sam followed the leader?

"Sir? Is everything okay?" Maddie asked, who was now staring at the expert sitting next to Sam.

Sam tilted his head up toward Maddie, and then turned his head toward the expert. The expert stared blankly back at him, and then slowly nodded his head. They were both on the same page. He was thinking the exact same thing as Sam was.

They had decoded the Morse code. They had found the leader. And now all they had to do was follow it. But Sam was torn. If his theory was correct, and the President of Pilgrim Tech was actually on board the Alpha Ship One, then letting the Alpha Ship One escape back into space was going to cause a rift between himself and Pilgrim Tech.

A rift that could end his life. If they found out that Sam could have stopped the President being taken from Earth's jurisdiction, then he'd be killed for his supposed act of treason.

But then again, what if the Alpha Ship One was trying to help them? What if the Alpha Ship One was about to reveal the location of the Annex Rebel Fleet? Was *one* President worth the risk? Did the math add up? Was the destruction of thousands of Earth's enemies worth more than the life of one man with absolute power?

Only time would tell. And Sam knew that time was not on their side.

"Sir? Is there something you're not telling me?" Maddie asked, her voice cracking as she spoke, her head dripping in sweat.

She was also in panic mode. And she sensed that there was something going on, something that she wasn't privy to.

The operational leader kept his cool. He looked up at her and smiled. It was the first genuine smile that he hadn't had to force in the past twenty-four hours. There wasn't much to smile about, but he felt like there was just enough to muster one joyous smile. Maybe, just maybe, they had their lead. A lead that came in the form of the Alpha Ship One. And maybe, just maybe, this would all be over before they knew it.

"Don't worry Maddie, we may be on to something here…" Sam said, his eyes locked onto his computer screen, following the Alpha Ship One as it began to leave Earth's atmosphere.

***

I was being flung back into my seat as the Alpha Ship One broke through Earth's outer crust. We were now in low orbit space. And the sudden yet slight change in G-force made my neck ache. The others – Philip and Teresa, along with Dale and the prisoner were all putting a brave face on.

The prisoner had woken up a few minutes prior, and refrained himself from asking any questions. When he saw the Pilgrim Tech President sitting next to him, a smile had crept across his face. He'd forgotten about the fact that Dale had smacked him in the back of the head, earlier. He'd also forgotten about the fact that he was onboard the Alpha Ship One, very much against his will. But he hadn't forgotten that we were all on a mission, and the mission was going to plan… so far.

So I guess that's why he had a smile on his face. And I also guess that's why I had one on mine as well. It had been a lot easier than I thought. Kidnapping the President of Pilgrim Tech had gone off without much of a hitch. You'd think that a building with that much security would be able to stop a mercenary ship from taking their most valuable asset into space, and pawning him off to a rebel alliance.

But I guess this wasn't a movie, and the bad guys are never as smart as they are usually portrayed to be. People make mistakes, and sure enough, there are always people - other people - to take advantage of those mistakes.

That's exactly what we were doing. We were taking advantage of Pilgrim Tech's mismanagement. We knew that they would be easily distracted by the battle going on above Earth's atmosphere. We also knew that the Commander and his rebels had gotten into their heads, and now things were personal. And whenever things become personal, war becomes easier. Battles are fought with bullets and brute force, not moral fiber.

Yet again, the movies of the past had made me think that in war, there were always two wildly different groups on opposing sides; one that was not afraid of doing whatever it took to win, and another that had a righteous and just cause behind their defense.

But this situation was nothing like that.

Even though I had decided to side with the rebels, I couldn't help but notice that both sides were as bad as each other. In my heart, I thought that humanity would never take the correct steps toward peace. Not when humans that opposed other humans were still willing to do whatever it took to win.

And just because a cause may seem right at the time, doesn't mean that stooping to the same level as the enemy was worthwhile. In my opinion, the idea of good versus evil is outdated. In reality, it's become a little more complicated. There are no good guys in this war. And there are no bad guys in this war. There are just people. And people, for good or bad, are usually the same.

"Wow, we actually did it!" The prisoner said from his chair, staring at the President of Pilgrim Tech who'd been gagged and bound in his seat.

The President wasn't mumbling, nor was he resisting. He'd come to terms with what was happening. But I assumed that he still had a lot of faith in his men to rescue him. After all, looking at the ship, I'd be in the same category of thinking as he was.

The Alpha Ship One was falling apart. The crew weren't exactly upstanding citizens. And putting those two things together, I wouldn't be surprised if he thought that we didn't stand a chance at succeeding in our goal. But then again, the people at the top usually underestimate the people at the bottom.

That's how revolutions come about.

"Don't get too ahead of yourself there, we still have to get to your planet. So I suggest you sit back, shut your mouth, and hope we don't get blasted to bits in the middle of this battle," I said, steering the ship toward the dogfight that was taking place on the cusp of Earth's atmosphere.

"Before Big Man over here knocked me out, I took the initiative and punched in the coordinates to our planet. They should be logged in onto your homing system. Just press option two, and the ship should route you toward the stronghold," the prisoner said.

I nodded my head, and turned toward my computer system. I did as he said, and to my surprise, he was telling the truth. I pressed option two, and watched as the ship's navigation system showed me a routing map toward the planet.

The mysterious rebel planet lay on the edge of the Milky Way Galaxy, and if I was going to be able to get there within the next day, I'd have to warp toward it. But warping was going to be a little difficult with my current set of circumstances. There was a battle waging on in front of me, a battle I didn't want no part of.

Luckily, on our way toward the planet earlier, I'd managed to scrape myself past without attracting any attention. But now, now there were many more Snake Pit Fighters fighting against the rebels. And I feared that there were far too many of them to sneak on by safely this time.

I began to panic as I sat there in my chair. The floor beneath me was vibrating as the ship's engines roared. I close my eyes for a few seconds, and tried to imagine myself on the outside of the ship, standing on top of it with a pair of binoculars, trying to scout the best possible pathway toward safety.

My problem was that the battlefield was now mixed with many more different ships. There was no longer a clear divide between the rebel ships and Earth's defense ships. They had all been stirred together like a broth, intertwining around each other like branches in a tree.

I had to find the clearest pathway so I could get my crew and my ship as far away from danger as possible. But everywhere I looked, there was obstacle after obstacle. So I would have to think fast if I wanted to get the President of Pilgrim Tech out of Earth's jurisdiction. But the longer I sat there in my chair, contemplating the options that stood in front of me, the less likely victory would be.

I needed a clear head. But I couldn't ascertain one with so many distractions. Or with so much danger. I was buckling under my own pressure. Pressure I'd put on myself to succeed. Not only had I turned my back on my own people, but I was now putting my ship, and my crew up against insurmountable odds.

"Don't just sit there doing nothing, get us out of here!" The prisoner yelled from his seat.

"There's too many of them. If I even attempt to enter the fray, I fear that we won't last more than two seconds. We need to think more objectively. We cannot rush this. We only have one chance, one shot, to get this right. If we mess this up, then there's no turning back. All of us will hang for what we've done!" I said, momentarily turning in my chair to face the others.

I was searching their faces for moral support. But all I got back from them was confusion. They were confused as to why I had all of a sudden lost my confidence. And I guess it was my fault really. I had tried to portray the fact that I was certain in my decision to associate myself with the rebels and do their bidding, that I hadn't taken the time to figure out whether I was truly ready to pull off such a coup.

But the prisoner was right. I didn't have the luxury of time, and sitting there worrying about the *what ifs* of this campaign wasn't going to do me any good. So I made a decision. A decision to act. And I was going to act as fast and as effectively as I could.

"Fuck it, strap yourselves in, hold tight, and hope for the best. I'm shooting for the stars," I said, buckling myself in, and breathing through my nose.

I stared at the screen in front of me, and momentarily calculated the odds of failure. I kept my calculations to myself. If I even uttered a single truth of what I'd just mathematically worked out, then I thought that my men and women would lose all hope. Because truthfully speaking, there wasn't much hope left.

I had dug myself into a hole. A hole that I feared was so deep I'd risk falling out of the other end. But I didn't know where this hole would take me. I had the best intentions at heart, but at the end of the day, those intentions weren't going to win us a revolution. Only willpower and bravery would. So I would have to be brave.

I punched the accelerator on the Alpha Ship One, and watched as the ship dipped slightly. The nose of the ship pointed downwards for a few seconds, and then came bobbing back up like a flotation device. The ship would automatically steer itself toward the coordinates that had been installed on the navigation module - coordinates that the prisoner had given me. Coordinates to his planet - a planet where we were scheduled to land with the Pilgrim Tech President in our custody.

So I didn't need to do much - all I had to do was get us past this battle. I pushed the accelerator to a hundred percent, and maxed the engine power as well. The ship rattled from left to right as the engines shook violently within their housing chambers. I could hear the engines moan and groan as I put the ship through its paces.

The battle in front of us was getting nearer. Flashes of light glared through the portholes on either side of the Alpha Ship One. It had a disorientating effect. It was as if we were at some sort of dance party, the lights flashing on and off, like strobe lighting. But this wasn't a party. Nor was this a dance. This was a war zone. And the lights were emanating from ships being blown up. Some of those ships were Earth ships. Others were rebel ships. But I was only focusing on making sure that our ship didn't end up a flash of light as well.

I dipped the ship once again, the nose of the ship pointing downwards, trying to avoid a direct collision with some of the ships on the outskirts of the battle. None of the ships had noticed us yet, nor had any of them tried to contact us. I knew that if any of the Earth ships ended up spotting us, then they would want answers as to why we were near a battle zone.

We were not a designated army ship, so we had no business being in their vicinity. I was just hoping that I could get away from the battle before it came to that. I wouldn't have the answers that the Snake Pit Fighters were looking for. And if I didn't have those answers, then they would have an answer of their own. They, after all, are known to follow protocol. Protocol states that an unidentified non-military ship that finds its way onto a battlefield can be deemed as hostile by the Earth Defense League.

So the stakes were high. So high in fact that I'd already made two mistakes. The first mistake was not cloaking the ship. And quite frankly, it was the biggest mistake of all. The second mistake was thinking too much. And in thinking too much, I had allowed the first mistake to on slip by, and before I knew it, it was too late to rectify.

"Shit, I forgot to cloak!" I said out loud, more to myself than anybody else. But I knew it was too late.

As the Alpha Ship One passed the crest of the battle, I saw two Snake Pit Fighters in the distance. And unlike the other Snake Pit Fighters, they were not facing the enemy. They were facing us. And I knew this was it. They'd spotted us. The gig was up. The game was over. It was too late to turn back now. I had to deal with whatever was about to happen.

"They've spotted us. I repeat, they have spotted us. Dale, saddle up on the gunner's seat, and take aim. If they fire on us, I want to at least be able to defend against it."

Dale grunted, and I could hear him readying up the weapons. We had two distinct weapon modules onboard. One of them was a laser weapon. It was short range. And the other was a cannon system. That was long-range.

But I wouldn't mistake my ship as a battleship. It was a haulage ship. It had the capability of defending itself against possible piracy, but it certainly didn't stand up against a military vessel. And the two Snake Pit Fighters in front of me, the ones that had spotted me, they were military grade. Their ships were outfitted with hundreds of mechanisms, mechanisms that had the unique purpose of destroying vessels of all sizes.

So it was safe to say that I was absolutely terrified.

"Captain, we are getting a hail from one of the Snake Pit Fighters in front. It's on the emergency channel. I suggest you answer it, or we won't be breathing in the next two seconds," Philip said, who was seated at the comms desk.

I raised my hand in the air, and signaled him to allow the hail to come through. Within the blink of the eye, I was face-to-face with one of the Snake Pit Fighters. The video-calling mechanism had been turned on. And we were now both staring at each other. He was wearing a combat helmet fitted with a visor that covered the majority of his face.

All I could see of him was his teeth. And they were gritted. It was obvious to me that he was nervous. Nervous that I was a rebel. I could see the reflection of his ship's command console on his visor. And in that reflection I could see that he had a lock-on on our ship. My heart began to beat incredibly fast in my chest.

I could feel the sweat dripping down my face. The hairs on my neck were standing on end. And a ringing was sounding off in my ear. I suppressed the urge to beg for mercy. I didn't want him to think I was the enemy.

And truth be told, I was not.

I had no interest in destroying his ship. All I wanted to do was get as far away from the battle as possible. But I didn't think that would hold up as a good defense. So I quickly flicked through my brain like a Rolodex. I was trying to find the right answer to this situation. Not that I knew what the actual situation was yet. He hadn't said anything. But I knew that whatever he was about to say would not be favorable toward me, or my ship. And it didn't take long for that assumption to become true.

"Alpha Ship One, this is Snake Pit Fighter 767. You are entering an active battlefield. If you do not turn around and return to Earth, then I will have no choice but to destroy your ship. Do you understand?" The pilot said, his teeth still gritted, the reflection of the lock-on he had on us still visible on his tinted black visor.

I had to think fast. I couldn't stutter. I needed to answer him. But I didn't know what to say. Luckily, Philip had zoomed the camera into my face. He couldn't see the goings-on directly behind me. He couldn't see the Pilgrim Tech President bound and taped up to the chair. He couldn't see the rebel soldier sitting next to him. Because if he could see that, he wouldn't be talking to me now.

But then I had a brainwave. What if it wasn't too late? What if it was just the right time? The right time to cloak the ship? The right time to disappear? The right time to get the hell out of sight?

"Cloak activated," I said, the expression on the pilot's face quickly changing.

I heard an alarm sound off within his cockpit. The lock-on was no longer activated. He'd lost sight of me. And he knew it. But he could still see me on the screen. My face staring back at him. And he'd heard exactly what I'd said.

He took a punt. He decided to fire, noticing that I hadn't manually turned the ship yet. A missile fired straight at us. But I'd hit supercruise mode at the same time that I'd activated cloak mode.

The missile missed. One second we'd been right in front of him, and the next we were two miles past him. The Alpha Ship One shot through the battle, flying underneath the waging warships. I quickly turned the face-to-face camera off, and disengaged communications with the Snake Pit Fighter.

"They are following us!" Philip shouted.

But I was way ahead of them.

Super cruise mode allowed us to shoot past the battle in half a minute. We had cleared over forty-eight miles within those thirty seconds. The Alpha Ship One was no longer in the heart of the battle, and we were now gaining pace, leaving the other ships behind us in our proverbial rearview. I noticed that the two Snake Pit Fighters were indeed still following us. But the ship was cloaked, so they wouldn't be able to ping our location.

I knew that once we reached a certain threshold of seventy-five miles north of the battle, then I could hit warp drive once again. But we still had around ten seconds before that could be accomplished. And ten seconds was plenty enough time to get caught out by the Snake Pit Fighters that were on our tail.

As I said before, their ships had magnificent capabilities. And if they got close enough, the cloaking device on my ship wouldn't stop them from pinpointing us. I was pretty sure that at that very moment in time the pilot was engaging his inferred sensors. If he activated those sensors, and got close enough to us, he'd be able to catch the heat signals coming from the Alpha Ship One.

And if he was able to pinpoint the exact location of our ship, he'd be able to get a lock-on once again, and end our mission before it even began. Not only would it end our mission, but it would also end our lives. I was certain of it. So I had to come up with an alternative to permanent death.

"Philip, EMP his ass!" I said.

I heard Phillips' voice crack, as if he was about to disagree with my order, but then I also heard the unmistakable sound of the Alpha Ship One hitting the two Snake Pit Fighters behind us with a blast wave.

That blast wave would, in hindsight, give our position away, but at the same time, it would also disable the electronics onboard the two Snake Pit Fighter ships. Their electrics would be out for a few seconds, but it would be a valuable two seconds nonetheless. We would have enough time to reach the threshold, and hit warp drive. And unless the Snake Pit Fighters were willing to warp drive along with us, then we would be safe.

A big ship like the Alpha Ship One had the ability to sustain warp drive for a lot longer than a fighter ship like the Snake Pit Fighters behind us. Their ships were smaller, yet more effective in the battlefield, while the Alpha Ship One was built with defense in mind.

It's what it did best. Running away, as fast as it could, to another star, to safety. For a long time, I had dreamt of flying a battlecruiser – a ship capable of destroying anyone that comes across it. But after many close shaves with other ships, I've come to the conclusion that the Alpha Ship One will do me just fine.

"Ready to warp," Teresa said from her console.

We reach the threshold, and I activated warp drive. The Alpha Ship One un-cloaked, revealing itself for a few seconds, before it melded into the blackness of space, and disappeared within the blink of an eye.

We were now one step closer toward the rebel's planet. One step closer to victory…

Chapter Twelve

The Commander of the Annex Rebel Fleet emerged from the elevator feeling positive. He had been told that his underground scientists had hit a breakthrough in their mission directive. The elevator he had just walked out of had been built to reach an underground bunker he had constructed on the rebel planet. It was a bunker that he hoped the humans would never find if they landed on his planet.

For that was the plan. Draw them out, direct them toward his planet, and wait for the rest to fall into place. If he was going to stand a chance of defeating Earth, then he would need them to fight him and his people on his terms. A battle against Earth Defense League wasn't going to be winnable in an environment that the humans were used to. To win against a battle-hardened enemy, victory could only be attained on unfamiliar ground. And the rebel planet that he held like a chess piece in his arsenal, was definitely unfamiliar ground.

Earth and its people had no idea that it even existed, let alone what its purpose was. The Alpha Ship One was the key to drawing them toward the planet. He had managed to convince the captain and its crew that they would be playing a vital part in this revolution. And even though that was partly true, the Commander was leaving out an integral piece of information.

The president of Pilgrim Tech was bait. And when trying to catch something big or small, the juicier the bait is, the easier the catch will be. Luckily for the Commander, the rebels had managed to dangle the juiciest bait of all. And now that they had their live bait, they could progress with their mission. The true mission.

A mission that not even the majority of his men knew about.

He was serious about winning this war. He was serious about defeating Earth and its corrupt government. So serious in fact, he was willing to give away the location of his trump card. That trump card was the planet he was on right now. The people back on Earth, the ones trying to stop him in his crusade would be so distracted by the possibility of obtaining the location of the rebel planet, that they would be blinded, so blinded in fact, that they wouldn't even be able to tell that it was all a trap to begin with.

Bait and switch – one of the oldest plays in the book of war. And it looked as if it was working just fine. They were tracking the Alpha Ship One. Just like he'd planned. The crew of the Alpha Ship One did not know it, but they too had a mole onboard their ship. And that mole was the prisoner, the prisoner that they had kept alive.

The prisoner had installed a decryption device on the computer system onboard the vessel. Its job was simple, it would decrypt the signal emanating from the ship, and ping it toward Earth. It would attempt to rouse the suspicion of the controllers back on planet Earth, and the way it would do that would be by sending out a Morse code communications module.

Earth would wonder what the significance of that Morse code meant, and all eyes would be on the Alpha Ship One. Putting that together with the fact that the Alpha Ship One was harboring the President of Pilgrim Tech, then all resources would be diverted toward the ship, and apprehending it. But Commander Korr knew that the Alpha Ship One was good enough to shake off any attempts at capture. That is why the Commander chose the Alpha Ship One. And that is why he knew that they would successfully lead planet Earth and its forces toward the cloaked planet, a cloaked planet where a big surprise was awaiting the soldiers of Pilgrim Tech.

The Commander walked down the underground maze system toward the scientist's layer. The underground complex that the

Commander had commissioned was large and efficient. Everywhere he turned, people worked tirelessly in bringing to life the vision that he had for his revolution. The majority of the fighters that the Commander governed had no idea of the true extent of the power that the Annex Rebel Fleet had.

If they'd known the true power at their disposal, then maybe they wouldn't be so willing to lay their lives down on the line to fight Earth and its Snake Pit Fighters. For the Commander knew that the vessels he had sent out to fight Earth and its defenses were merely cannon fodder. He wanted Earth to grow confident in knowing that the rebels didn't pose much of a threat. They would grow so confident in fact that they would be willing to jeopardize the safety of their planet by diverting all of their resources toward the rebel planet. And when they did that, then his master plan would come to fruition.

A plan that the Commander was so proud of that he couldn't help but grin as he walked into the scientist's lab and confronted the lead scientist that'd been working on his secret project.

"I take it that everything is going well down here?" The Commander asked.

His voice startled the scientist, making the frail old man turn on his heels to face his ferocious leader. But he didn't have fear in his eyes, no, not at all, he had excitement and jubilation smeared across his mug.

While others were frightened of Commander Korr, this particular scientist was infatuated. He couldn't quite believe that this little plan of his was working. Not only was it working, but it was borderline perfect! It was a plan that was sure to cause ripple effects across the Universe. So no, the scientist was not afraid, but he was happy. Beyond happy. Happy that Pilgrim Tech were about to pay for their sins.

"Yes sir, the cloning is at 99%. The other one percent should take no longer than two hours to complete. And once that's done, then the rest is up to you," the scientists said, holding a clipboard in both his hands, admiring the statistics on the paper attached to the clipboard.

"Good, I'm glad that we're making such progress. Inform the others that they are on their way. Soon, Earth will know the true extent of our power. And once they see it, they will bow down to their rightful leaders – us, the Annex Rebel Fleet," the Commander said.

The scientist nodded his head emphatically. The Commander was correct. Earth would soon know the true extent of their power. And once they found out what the rebels had been cloning, there's no doubt that public favor toward the rebels would increase.

A revolution like this was all about the numbers. Numbers that can override society – a society woven with corruption – a society destined to succumb to the numbers – it was simple mathematics, really.

***

I got up from my seat and stretched my legs. We were still warping toward the rebel planet, and judging by the estimated time of arrival left on the computer screen, I had an hour or so to think things through more clearly. This whole situation felt like it had occurred out of the blue.

No less than twenty-four hours ago I was onboard Sector Eight, minding my own business, enjoying my life, getting ready to re-enter the field. And then this happened. And it happened fast. It all kind of felt like a blur to me. A smudge in reality. A smudge that I couldn't wipe clean. A smudge that I had to deal with. But truth be told, I had no idea how to deal with this. I was having second thoughts already. And what was making the second thoughts even more prevalent was the fact that my crew hadn't uttered as much as a single word to me about this ordeal since we'd welcomed the President of Pilgrim Tech on board.

Maybe they were having second thoughts as well. I hadn't really given them an opportunity to voice their own opinion, let's not forget. I'd decided for the majority of us that we should consider siding with the rebels. And it was a decision that I would have to live with. But it got me thinking; was it a decision that they would have to live with as well?

Couldn't they just put the proverbial white flag up and wave it in the air, switching allegiances from me and the rebels to just themselves? It was a very real possibility, a possibility that I wasn't ready to confront in my mind. I didn't want to lose Teresa. I certainly didn't want to lose Dale or Philip. They all meant a great deal to me.

But just because I was the captain of the ship, didn't mean that I could dictate the fate of my three amigos. Once we reached the planet, I had a feeling that it would be every man for himself. The rebel leader, Commander Korr, hadn't exactly promised anything to us. We didn't know what was waiting for us on that planet. And we certainly didn't know what was waiting for us back on Earth. So some time to think was definitely valuable at a time like this.

"Take his gag out," I said, walking up toward the President of Pilgrim Tech, who's still tied to his chair.

Dale was standing next to him, like a brick wall, not daring to move until my command had been voiced. I watched as Dale took the President's gag out of his mouth, and stuffed it in his own pocket. The guy was wearing an immaculate suit, and had a little brooch pinned to his lapel. I was transfixed by the brooch, and wondered how much it was worth. That, after all, was my way of thinking. I had a habit of putting a monetary value on everything. It was most likely the reason why I got into this line of work in the first place. In my field, money talked, and it also made you walk. It took you to places that many could only dream of. And from the very first day that I got this ship, I dreamt of making some serious money.

Luckily, I had succeeded. But at the same time, I was a broken man. And what use is money to a broken man? It can't buy you happiness. And it certainly can't buy you your freedom, I know that all too well. So what could money buy you in this day and age of space travel? Not a lot by the looks of it. Just ask the President of Pilgrim Tech, a man that has plenty of money, and now finds himself tied up to a chair onboard a mercenary ship about to sell him off to the enemy.

I wasn't stupid. There was a reason I was aligning myself with the rebels. And that reason was cash. I wanted plenty of it. Plenty of it to start a new life. A new life for me and Teresa. The Pilgrim Tech President was my ticket, my golden ticket to freedom. And I was about to announce my true intentions to the man himself.

"I guess you're wondering why you find yourself onboard the Alpha Ship One?" I said, staring intently into the President's eyes.

The guy that had brought him onto the ship was sat behind him, his head tilted toward the floor, minding his own business. I didn't know what to make of that guy. Part of me was frightened of him. The other part of me felt at ease around him. He seemed like the sort of man that only focused on his mission, and it was obvious that his mission was to get the President to the rebel planet. So if I stayed out of his way, I was pretty sure that he would stay out of ours.

"To be honest civilian, I don't really care," the President said, puckering his lips up into a grin.

"I don't care what your reasons for kidnapping me are. I don't care about your sorrowful story you are about to tell me. And I certainly don't care about the integrity of your men. The only thing I care about is the consequences that will be bestowed upon you once Earth finds out that you have everything to do with my kidnapping. And once they do find out, they too won't care about your reasoning behind what you did. All they will care about is spilling your blood and making you pay dearly. There is no getting out of this, Captain whoever you are. This is now very much your life. So get used to it. And please, don't bother wasting your time trying to explain yourself to me. It won't get you anywhere," the President said, still puckering his lips, still looking like a smartarse.

I stood there for a few seconds staring at the man. At first, I didn't quite know how to reply to his rhetoric. Although I was impressed with how cool, calm and collected he seemed, I wasn't impressed with his tone. And I thought that he needed to be brought back down to Earth, so to speak.

So I got as close to him as possible, and slapped him in the face. My crew weren't surprised by my tactics. They'd seen it before with the prisoner, the one sitting next to him. And the guy that brought the President in was still looking at the ground, uninterested in what I had to say. The Alpha Ship One continued to warp, and I continued to seethe, bending down, and going face-to-face with the President as he reeled in anger. It was obvious that he hadn't been physically touched in many years. Maybe he'd never been touched before. Maybe this was the first time that anybody had summoned the will and bravery to smack some sense into this son of a bitch.

And me being the first to do so brought a smile to my face. A smile that rivaled his previous grin.

"Well, President, you should care about the reason why you find yourself here onboard my ship. It boggles my mind that you cannot even remember who I am. Who we are. If you had any inkling as to who we were, you wouldn't be acting so smart right now would you? You'd be afraid of what I had in store for you. You'd be afraid of the consequences of your actions. Actions that cost a planet its species. And for what? To prove that you are the dominant one? Well, Mr. President, I hate to break it to you, but there's nothing dominant about you. What you do, and what you define as dominance, others see for what it truly is; and that's shooting fish in a fucking barrel. There is no skill or honor in what you do Mr. President. You are a dishonorable man. And dishonorable men need to be dealt with accordingly. We will deal with you, Mr. President. We will deal with you just fine, don't you doubt that. We have a plan for you. And ain't that plan glorious? Oh it is … it is glorious.

"I cannot wait to see your face when we touch down on the rebel planet, and I hand you over personally to a battalion of men that have a bone to pick with you. Because the Alpha Ship One isn't the only ship full of people you pissed off Mr. President. There's an army out there wanting your head on a pike, and I cannot wait to see them lop your head right off your damn shoulders. So continue to sit there with that stupid smile on your stupid face, thinking that the world cannot touch you because you come from money. That just because you have a few extra fucking zeros on your credit balance makes you untouchable… Don't you fucking dare think that you are getting out of this alive. You will pay for what you did. And your pals back home will also pay.

I took a deep breath and then started to laugh. The President squirmed in his seat as I chortled.

"You know what the best thing about this is? I'll get paid as well," I said, still standing face-to-face, pressing my cheek against his, foaming at the mouth as I spoke.

He looked at me with confusion in his eyes. It was as if he was trying to place my face. And then the penny dropped. He remembered. He remembered the day that he handed me and my crew a million credits each for our part in their forced war. He remembered the fact that I lost the majority of my original crew because of his heinous act. He also remembered what I said to him when I walked out of that room. *That my lips were sealed. That this was all forgotten about.*

But how wrong he was…

"This is what this is all about? Those damn Ursines? You are seriously risking the livelihood of your people, your crew, for fucking space bears? Are you kidding me? Do you seriously expect me to believe that you are doing this as a form of revenge? Don't kid yourself Capt. Flynn, I know who you are and who your damn crew of misfits are. And I know that the only thing you care about is cold hard cash. So don't kid yourself, you aren't doing this because you are the better man, you are doing this because you are the greedier man," the President said, saliva dripping down his chin as he gnashed his teeth while he spoke.

His face had gone completely red. And he was seeing red at that. I had gotten to him. I had accomplished my goal. He was scared. And he remembered. Remembered who the hell he was talking to. No matter what he said, I knew that deep down, he knew he was in the wrong. And he also knew that he would pay dearly for what he did to me, my crew, the deceased that had worked on the ship, and the Ursines that he had double-crossed.

I didn't need to hear any more of his excuses.

"Gag the motherfucker, I don't need to hear another boldfaced lie," I said, Dale immediately obeying my order and stuffing the gag back into the President's mouth.

I turned back around, and walked toward my chair. Standing next to it was Philip. I was surprised to even see him, especially since he'd been more or less avoiding me for the past hour or so. I didn't need to hear him speak to know that he had a lot on his mind. His facial expression said it all. But I allowed him to voice his concerns nonetheless as I sat down in my chair, and tried to smile at my friend.

"You meant all that?" Philip asked.

I nodded.

"Yeah, I did. This isn't about joining the rebels. Not for me at least. You, Teresa and Dale can do as you please once we land on their planet. But the only thing that I want from this is retribution. I want that cocksucker to pay for what he did to us. For what he did to Raj and Jess. How he forced us to do their dirty work. How they marooned us on that godforsaken planet. They need to pay for what they did, Philip. And I'd understand if you didn't want anything to do with me or my ship once this is all said and done. I'm not asking you to join the rebels, I'm asking you to join the Alpha Ship One. I'm asking you to be part of my crew, a crew that can do as it pleases and isn't held back by the government, a government that has screwed me over far too many times for me to forgive them," I said.

Philip was leaning against my command console. At first, his facial expression had been hard and un-trusting. But now, his features had softened slightly.

"If you are telling the truth, and this is actually about what happened on the Ursine planet, then I have no choice but to stand by your side. Teresa feels the same. And I know Dale is as loyal as they come. So don't worry about us, Capt. Flynn. Don't worry about us leaving you, and going our own separate ways. We are a team. And you are our trusted navigator. If you have a vision, a grand plan, for our ship, for our families, then who are we to stop you? I trust you - we all do. I just hope that we can trust the rebels," Philip said, still leaning against my command console.

I nodded my head, and stood back up. I put my hand out toward Philip and he shook it. We then embraced each other in a hug.

"I can only hope that we haven't gotten ourselves into something we cannot get out of," I said, releasing Philip's hand, and grabbing his shoulder. "But I can promise you Philip if the rebels aren't being truthful about their intentions, Pilgrim Tech won't be the only group to pay for their misdeeds."

Chapter Thirteen

Operational leader Sam was facing his co-workers. This was a big moment for him, a moment that he had been building up to for the past hour or so. Things had changed dramatically. Everything had gone to pot. And if he wasn't quick and decisive in his actions, then he and his fellow workers would pay dearly for his own mistakes.

The biggest mistake he had made so far was following his gut. His gut had told him to keep the developments about the Alpha Ship One under wraps, and in essence, run a separate reconnaissance mission on the vessel without the help of his office workers. If he had decided to ignore his gut feeling, then maybe the Pilgrim Tech President would still be in his office, safe and sound, and the stalemate between the rebels and Earth would continue.

But instead, hundreds of human ships had been destroyed, and thousands of rebels had died. So much blood had already been spilled, and operational leader Sam wasn't sure how much more bloodletting could go on before society as he knew it would implode. So he had taken the decision to address the men and women in his office, and tell them about the mysterious Alpha Ship One, and how he suspected the President of Pilgrim Tech was onboard. Luckily for Sam, he had already informed the Snake Pit Fighter regiment that the Alpha Ship One was their sole priority, and ninety-five percent of Earth's available fleet were tailing the ship, a few thousand miles behind, close enough to stay on radar, but far enough for the Alpha Ship One to not suspect a single thing.

"Can I have everybody's attention?" Sam said, standing at the helm of his desk, staring at the men and women that were working tirelessly at their computer terminals.

As if in sync, they all stopped working, and turned to face their boss. Judging by the expressions on their faces, Sam knew that they knew something was going on. Something big, something significant.

But unfortunately, they didn't have the luxury of knowing that their job was already done. Pilgrim Tech wouldn't need them anymore, Sam was sure of it, but he needed them to know the full extent of what was going on, so they could at least die knowing that it wasn't all for nothing.

Sam was pessimistic about their chances of survival, not that he would be telling them that. He was well aware that his workers knew the gravity of working for Pilgrim Tech, and he didn't take them for fools. Once they had heard what Sam had to say, he hoped that they would make the right decision by themselves, a decision whether to abandon their posts, or continue the fight for a corporation that saw them as numbers.

Numbers that had to be subtracted after such a grand failure, the grandest failure of them all, the failure of not seeing the rebels coming, the failure of not keeping their President safe, the failure of letting the rebels slip past them, their leader onboard, most likely already dead, and there was nothing that they did to stop it.

"Okay, I'd like everybody to stop what they're doing, and just listen to what I have to say. Unfortunately, it has come to my attention that the kidnappers that took the President have been on our radar for the past fifteen hours. The suspected ship that took the President has been identified as the Alpha Ship One. For some reason, it caught my eye yesterday evening, and I decided to put a tracker on it, not knowing the full extent of what the ship had planned, or that it was about to see its plan through. I decided to keep that information to myself, and only a few of my closest allies in this office knew about the Alpha Ship One, but no one but me knew of its significance. Granted, the only thing I had to go on by was a gut feeling, a gut feeling telling me that the Alpha Ship One was up to something.

"As many of you know, gut feelings aren't concrete. So, I suppose it is understandable that I didn't feel it necessary to burden you with the knowledge that I held. But I'm afraid that decision has come back to haunt me. I am now a hundred percent certain that the Alpha Ship One is not only an undercover rebel ship, but it is the vessel responsible for the kidnap of our President. When news breaks out that this office had a tracker on the ship, and suspected it of ill will, the people above will blame us for this mishap. I just hope that the majority of you understand why I did what I did, because just in the same light as suspecting the ship of having rebel ties, and it being true, suspecting the ship of misdeeds and it not being true would be just as harsh for us, consequences wise.

"They would blame me and you for wasting resources on a ship that had nothing to do with the kidnapping. That is why I kept quiet on the matter. But I cannot keep quiet anymore, and all of you should know the true extent of what is going on. These rebels seem to be serious about their endeavor. They are well equipped, and could quite possibly overtake Earth's defenses. It seems as if they have a rebel planet somewhere in the Milky Way Galaxy, and right now, the Alpha Ship One is making its way toward that planet. When I started to piece things together, I also decided to inform Pilgrim Tech of my mistake. I assured them that you guys had nothing to do with my blunder. But they were not interested in excuses, and only want results. So I told them that I had instructed every available ship in our fleet to tail the Alpha Ship One, until it reaches its destination.

"When the Alpha Ship One reaches the planet, our ships will reveal themselves, and hopefully catch the rebels by surprise. I've sanctioned a shoot to kill mission on the planet, meaning that every rebel that our fleet comes across will be blown to pieces. If everything goes to plan, the rebel contingent will be destroyed. And if that does indeed happen, then my blunder would have also saved Earth from certain annihilation. So, I hope with all my heart that I have done enough to secure both our jobs and our lives. And I also hope that all of you can forgive me for my mistake, but I'm still holding out hope that the mistake I made will actually result in the biggest victory of our existence," operational leader Sam said, still standing over his desk, still staring at his fellow co-workers.

Nobody said anything for a good solid minute. Everybody was taken back by the new information they found themselves privy to. Nobody in the office saw Sam as a bad person, but it was safe to say that some of them now had mixed feelings toward their leader. Everybody in that room knew how ruthless Pilgrim Tech was. And knowing that, they also knew how unforgiving they were.

"What if the rebels win? What if this is a trap? What do we do then?" Maddie said, from her desk not daring to look at her boss, feeling guilty about challenging his view on their current situation.

Sam didn't answer straight away. He just stared down at his computer screen, and followed the Alpha Ship One on the schematic map. It was nearing what he assumed to be its final destination. Some of the geeks in the back room had estimated the ship's bearing, and with that information, operational leader Sam knew that things were about to come to a head. The only thing that operational leader Sam didn't know, was how to answer his friend, his colleague, Maddie.

But he had to answer her, or risk looking weak in front of the others. At a time like this, answers were needed, and he would have to be the man to provide those answers.

"If the rebels win, then we win. I am fully aware of who we work for, but let's not beat around the bush here people, if Pilgrim Tech beat the rebels, then we will suffer. It was, after all, us that allowed such a travesty to happen. At least, that is how they will see things. So, maybe we have to ask ourselves something here; would it be that bad for the rebels to be our masters? Is freedom such a bad thing?"

Nobody dared answer back. These were dangerous times, and operational leader Sam was walking a very dangerous line, a line that there would be no coming back from.

All he could do was hope that on the other end of the line, there was freedom for his family and his co-workers. He was tired of being threatened. Tired of being forced to do things that he didn't want to do. So maybe it wasn't so bad that the rebels might win. But then again, who's to say that a rebel alliance government wouldn't subject its people to the same harsh reality that Pilgrim Tech reigns down on them each and every day?

Sometimes a person's worst enemy is themselves. The grass is never greener on the other side. But then again – green grass is overrated.

***

I couldn't quite believe it, but we had arrived. The rebel planet stood right in front of us, floating in the distance, both gorgeous and glorious at the very same time. I knew that we had arrived because the prisoner had told me to slow down. He'd also told me to punch in a code into my computer's communication system. He informed me that the code I was punching in was an access code to the planet, and it was supposed to reveal the planet, in turn uncloaking it.

The code I had put in worked. And the planet was now fully visible – before resembling a rippling sphere of water, but now bright and solid with color. I was transfixed by its beauty, and at the same time, nervous to know that on it, on its surface, was danger.

Clear and complete danger. A danger aimed at my planet, and my people. But it was a danger I was planning to overcome. Let's not forget, I was the one in the driver's seat, both figuratively and metaphorically. I was the one that had the President of Pilgrim Tech onboard my vessel. So in my opinion, I was the one that held the cards in this game of poker we were playing.

My cards were high and suited and booted. To be honest, it could be aces and eights, or a Royal flush. It didn't really matter, because I had the King. And the king was forever mine, until I got what I wanted from the rebels. So I wasn't as worried as I probably should have been. In fact, I was more or less excited. Excited to be part of history. Because I knew that these rebels, these Annex Rebel Fleet chaps, they were serious. And I was just as serious as they were in my collective hate toward Pilgrim Tech and everything it stood for.

So I figured that we would have a good relationship from now on. And even though I didn't plan on joining their contingent, I knew deep down that I was firmly a member in spirit. I was hoping that further in the future, maybe our paths would cross again, and if they did, then maybe great things would occur. But I was living in reality, and right now, right at that very moment, the only thing I cared about, was holding up my end of the bargain. I just hoped that they too would hold up theirs.

"Approaching fast, everybody make sure that they are strapped in," I said, steering the ship gently toward the planet.

To my surprise, as we got closer, and the planet expanded in front of us, I could now see thousands of warships. My heart began to flutter in my chest. At first, I thought that the ships belonged to Earth, and this was a trap, and somehow they had gotten ahead of us, and found out our true intentions.

But then, as my ship neared, I recognized the vessels in front of me. They were rebel ships. Large and hulking in their presence, I was absolutely mystified by the sheer numbers that surrounded me. I knew that these rebels were serious, and they had some impressive firepower, but I didn't know that they themselves were basically a planetary force, a force that no doubt could stand strong and tough against our own fleet back home.

Suddenly, I felt nervous. Was I the proverbial chicken house, and they the proverbial Fox? Was this a trap concocted by the dastardly Commander that I had spoken to earlier? Had I fallen for something here, thinking that the actual danger we faced was from Pilgrim Tech and not from the rebels? Whatever the case may be, it was far too late to have second thoughts. This was done, and I had done it. And now, the Alpha Ship One was approaching their planet, so technically, our fate was very much in their hands.

"What have you done? Can you not see the danger you have put our people in?" The President of Pilgrim Tech said.

I immediately turned around in my chair, and saw that he had managed to spit out his gag. I told Dale to shut him up. Dale did exactly as I said, and stuffed the gag deep into his gob. I turned back around to face my controls, and sighed. I didn't have the patience or fortitude to listen to the ramblings of the President. He was biased. This was very much about him, and I expected him to be defensive. But I couldn't help but think that maybe he was right. Maybe I'd made a mistake here. Maybe Earth would suffer for my split-second decision. A decision that would affect our planet for generations to come. This was a serious situation. And I had a bad feeling about this. But it wasn't like I could just turn back around, and get the hell out of dodge now, was it?

The thousands of warships that had greeted us were making sure that I didn't run. They were an insurance policy. And I'd be stupid to think that they were anything less than that. Why else would there be so many of them? Unless they figured that we had been followed.

Maybe they thought that Earth was on our tail? But I hadn't picked up any anomalies on the radar. But then again, cloaking technology wasn't exclusive to rebel planets or hundred-year-old rust buckets like the Alpha Ship One.

So maybe I'd been a little naive.

"Alpha Ship One, this is Annex Rebel Fleet control, please slow down, and follow our fleet, they'll take you to your landing spot on our planet, and then our Commander will meet up with you. We hope you had a pleasant journey," a voice on my radio said.

I burst out laughing, I didn't mean to, and thankfully I wasn't on radio chatter, so the so-called Annex Rebel Fleet control didn't hear me cackling. But I couldn't help it. How absurd! Why on earth would they have hoped that I had a pleasant journey? Do they not know who I have onboard? Or what I had to do to get that man onboard? There was nothing pleasant about what I had done. And if they thought that they could convince me otherwise, they were surely mistaken.

But I had to keep on keeping on, and that's exactly what I did – I kept close to the warships in front of me as they guided me into the planet's atmosphere. This was officially the fifteenth planet that I had visited in my career as a captain onboard the Alpha Ship One. And this was also officially the second planet I had visited because of Pilgrim Tech.

The first planet I had visited because of them was the Ursine planet, and it was by force. But this planet, this planet was different. It was also because of Pilgrim Tech, but nobody had forced me to go here. I had chosen to. And at least I had that going for me. At least I had my dignity and my integrity. I was no longer being pushed about by a government forcing me to do their dirty work.

This was all me. And I was proud of that, if not a little rattled and shaken. Because deep down, I feared the worst. Deep down, I was frightened; frightened that I had fallen for the same trick twice. Frightened that they had made me do their bidding, and I was now in effect the Annex Rebel Fleet's go to paperboy.

"Dale, I suggest you stay frosty, I have a bad feeling about this," I said, turning in my chair to face my trusted gunner. I then looked at Philip and Teresa, who also looked worried.

"I wouldn't worry about it, Flynn," an unfamiliar voice said, that voice was coming from the man that had brought the President on board my ship. I'd almost forgotten about him, seeing that he hadn't said a single word since stepping on the ship. But now he was smiling at me. And he was no longer looking at the floor. I could now see his eyes clearly, and they were filled with hate.

I suddenly knew the gravity of what I had just done.

"It will be just fine, Capt. Flynn. You did your people proud. And now the world will know the true ferocity of the Annex Rebel Fleet," the man said.

I tried to ignore the feeling of impending doom bubbling in the pit of my stomach. But it was useless. I could feel the dread washing over me, as we entered the atmosphere of the rebel planet. Before I knew it, we were no longer in space, but were now hovering over alien rocks and soil. The warships guided me toward a mass of ships on the ground. From here, inside the Alpha Ship One, the massive ships looked like Lego toys. They were tiny and minuscule, but as we got closer, the true size of the rebel army became apparent.

"Holy shit, what have I done?" I said, seeing the Army of rebels below. I couldn't quite make them out, but then the ships beside me started to land, and I also proceeded to do the same.

As the Alpha Ship One touched the rebel planet's soil, I was left shocked at the sheer number of ships and troops around us. I couldn't make them out, but some of them didn't look human. And just as I was about to try to get a better look, I heard an air raid siren sounding off in the distance.

"What the hell is going on? How have you got this many troops?" I said, standing up and walking toward the mysterious man in the suit. He was now back looking at the floor, and I was just about to grab him by the scruff of the neck when the Alpha Ship One's side doors opened, and seven troops walked in.

"What's going on here? Where's the Commander?" I said, noticing that Dale had sidled up beside me, as if he was ready to protect me from the rebel troops.

But then I heard footsteps on the deck, heavy footsteps. The troops stepped aside, allowing the Commander to walk up toward me. He was a big man. A really big man, and he was holding a handgun. But he wasn't aiming it at me, he was aiming it at the President of Pilgrim Tech. The President was squirming in his chair, trying to scream, but the gag in his mouth didn't allow the screams to escape.

"What are you doing? We didn't bring him all this way just so you could…"

I was interrupted by the sound of a gunshot.

The large Commander had just shot the President of Pilgrim Tech in the head. Blood and brains soaked the chair in which he was sitting in, brain matter falling into his lap, his limp neck not able to hold the weight of his half split open skull.

"Jesus Christ!" I said, by now, I had my hands balled into fists.

But the Commander just smiled at me. He didn't say a single word, he just smiled while he held his gun, and pointed it at me.

And then he finally spoke.

"You did well, and that's the only reason I'm not going to kill you or your crew. Your mission was a success. And we thank you for it. Because without you, this couldn't have happened," the Commander said, the sound of the siren still wailing outside.

I was confused. I stood there staring at the Commander, and then frowned.

"You didn't need me to bring him all this way just so you could kill him. If you had someone working on the inside, surely you could have just done it yourself. So please, explain to me, why the hell did you want us to do this for you?" I said.

The Commander holstered his weapon. He then put his hands out to the sides, like he was gesturing at me to look around.

"Don't you hear the siren? Your job wasn't to bring the President of Pilgrim Tech here just so I could shoot him. Your job was to bring the Army of Earth to my planet so we could finally end this once and for all," the Commander said, turning around, quickly making his way toward the double doors. His entourage of troops followed.

"What are you on about? I didn't bring anyone here? It's just us," I said, and then the Commander turned back around, and smiled.

"They've been watching you, Capt. Flynn. They have a tracker on your ship. A tracker they have been following. And now that tracker has led them here. Shouldn't be too long now. And the best thing about it? You'll have a front-row seat to the end of the world," the Commander said, leaving through the double doors, and walking down on to the rebel planet's soil.

I looked down the ramp at the Commander as he walked off, and then at Philip and Teresa. The prisoner was still tied in this chair, but he had a smile on his face. Like he was in on this all along. The other man in the suit had slipped away by the looks of it. I just stood there, staring at my crew, wondering what the hell I just did.

"Whoo, here they come!" I heard somebody say outside.

I quickly ran toward the double doors and down the ramp and onto the surface. The ground beneath me was rocky and hard. It was a mixture of red dirt and sand. But it wasn't the ground beneath me that had caught my eye, but it was the Earth ships above me entering the planet's atmosphere, and making their way toward the rebels. No one opens fire yet, and I wondered why. Surely as soon as Earth's Snake Pit Fighters saw the rebels, they'd open up a can of serious whoop-ass on them. But that was not the case. They were distracted by something. And then I heard a roar.

"What the hell? It can't be..." Was all I could say.

***

The lead Snake Pit Fighter held onto his control sticks tightly. This was the moment that he had been waiting for. He and his men, a collective group of hundreds and thousands of ships of all sizes, had tracked down the rebels to their planet. Seconds ago, they were feeling both brave and strong. But now reality had settled in.

"You seeing this?" Somebody on his radio said.

He didn't answer back though. He was transfixed by what he was seeing; he didn't feel it necessary to discuss it with his fellow Snake Pit Fighters. They all had eyes. They all could see just as well as he could.

And what they were seeing was far from what they had expected.

Stretching for over ten miles on the ground were thousands of rebel ships, and they were all locked-on to the Earth's fleet as it entered the planet's atmosphere. But the ships weren't the worst of it. Behind them were hundreds of thousands of soldiers. At first, the lead Snake Pit Fighter thought that he was staring at a collective group of rebel members. But then, as he and his men got closer, he noticed that the soldiers he was staring at were not human.

They towered over some of the smaller ships next to them. They were big and bulky. And above all, they were ferocious. Snarling and biting at the air, the lead Snake Pit Fighter couldn't quite believe what he was seeing. He thought that they had been extinct. He thought that they no longer existed. But they did.

And now they were fighting for the rebels.

"Jesus Christ, are you guys seeing this? They have Ursines! Bloody Ursines!" The lead Snake Pit Fighter said, finally coming to terms with what was surely going to be the end of his existence.

The Ursines below roared as they swatted at the ships coming toward them. The Snake Pit Fighters were the first of Earth's offensive, but the Ursines was stopping them from striking, and in fact, all they could do was retreat.

Earth's fleet had gone into this thinking that they outnumbered the rebels. But it had come to their attention that the numbers game was firmly in the rebel's favor. Not only did the rebels have the numbers, but they now had the ground troops as well. And if Earth was going to survive the rebel onslaught, they'd need to get boots on the ground as soon as possible.

The game had changed. Earth were no longer the dominant force in the Milky Way Galaxy. They had a new foe to deal with. A foe that looked like them, acted like them, and fought like them. But

Earth's new-found foe had something that they themselves did not possess…

…A million strong Ursine army that was ready to rip their former tormentors to shreds.

To Be Continued…

Revenge of the Annex Rebel Fleet, book three in the Alpha Ship One series will be out on Kindle in the new year (2017). Catch the pre-order, exclusively on Kindle, January 1st 2017.

I hope that you enjoyed this book, if you did, please leave a review on Amazon. Reviews help me tremendously, and I love hearing what people think of my work.

Continue reading for a sample of Dropship One!

Thanks once again, you're a star!

X

Sample

I held the plasma railgun tightly in my grip. The troop carrier was shaking violently as we descended toward Tribeca's foreign soil. My stomach was in knots as I attempted to hold my dinner in. But it was no use, I was as green as the grass, and green was certainly how I felt. I leaned forward and hurled my guts up. A fountain of vomit escaped my gullet and sprayed all over the steel grated floor beneath me. My boots were covered in a carrot -like substance. The men around me groaned. I'd let them down. We were heading into battle and I'd already puked my guts up like the rookie I was.

"Rookie's gone chucked up his guts," one of my fellow Marines said.

But I didn't feel like a Marine. I felt like a failure. Like I'd jumped the gun and went into this headfirst without thinking. But now I was thinking. And I didn't know whether the fact that I'd just puked my guts up was playing havoc on my self-confidence, or I was now seeing things clearly; but now I didn't feel as confident as I did when I'd stepped on the troop carrier earlier on. Now, all my confidence was gone. There wasn't much left of me. Not much left in my stomach, or my heart. And I sensed that everybody around me felt exactly the same way. In the space of a few seconds, I'd become a shell of a man. The reality of war was crashing down on me much like the waves of bile in my stomach.

"Get a hold of yourself there Marine, puking your guts up isn't going to accomplish anything. Unless, the only thing you want to accomplish is getting chunks on your shiny shoes. But you seem like a bright young man, the type of young man that doesn't like to play with strands of vomit or mucus. I don't say this about many, but you don't seem half as retarded as some of the men that have graced this troop carrier in the past."

The men around me started to laugh. I wiped a smidgen of sick off my lips and looked up at who was talking to me. The guy continued his tirade. And I continued to suppress the explosive vomit in my stomach, holding it down to the best of my ability.

"So I'm giving you the benefit of the doubt and putting all this down to nerves. So sit up straight, breathe through your nose and puff your chest out like the son of a bitch I know you are," the Marine sergeant said to me as he flung his heavy arm around my shoulders and straightened me up a little.

I sat there with my chest puffed out, everybody else was looking at me, judging me, probably laughing at me – But I was here. I was here just like the rest of them. And just like the rest of them, I was here to make a difference. And that is exactly what we were going to do.

Make a difference.

"Thanks ever so much, Sir," I said to the Marine sergeant with his arm wrapped around my shoulder.

The man's tight grip loosened. He grunted, standing up and turning violently on his heels. His big abrasive boots screeched in protest as they made contact with the grated metal beneath his feet. The troop carrier continued to rattle and shake as it descended toward the foreign planet.

We'd all been briefed on our mission. It had all gone awry on the Tribeca planet. Something about merchant pirates becoming a little over friendly with the native population. The over friendliness soon turned into war. A war between two fierce alien species. But they weren't like us. They weren't anything like us humans. They didn't walk upright. They didn't speak an intellectual language. They were animals. And animals so often enjoyed animalistic behaviour. Savage beasts. But these beasts had been learning to get along with the rest of the Universe. Space and everything that surrounded it was teaming with all sorts of different creatures. Some were diplomatic. Others were violent and predatory.

Unfortunately, both the pirates and the natives of the Tribeca planet seemed to fall into the silent and predatory category. And we'd been sent there to stop the war escalating into an endgame event.

The thing is, it wasn't the natives of the Tribeca planet or the pirates I was worried about. I was sure they were going to fare quite well. But, we humans - Marines - weren't so favoured. In fact, instead of being revered, we were vilified. No planet nor its inhabitants wanted to see us landing on their soil. We only served one purpose, and that was protecting the merger of companies around the Universe. Companies that controlled the trade and market share of goods. And when a planetary event was deemed to be affecting the market negatively, the Marines were sent in to stabilise the market. And sometimes, the only way to stabilise anything was with pure carnage and violence.

The railgun in my hands signified carnage and violence well. It fired at a tremendous rate. Rounds and rounds skittering off into the horizon. Chances are my shots would hit something. And whatever it hit, it would bleed profusely. Yes, the railgun was the perfect weapon. A perfect weapon of violence. Carnage. Unadulterated death. At least my gun remained confident in my hands.

I knew that if my gun was a conscious being, it would be smiling right about now. Maybe even salivating at the thought of taking a creature's life. The gun would not have any problems with disembarking the ship, putting boots on the ground and searching for a viable target. It wouldn't have a problem pulling the trigger when the time was right. It wouldn't differentiate between male and female, man or beast, woman or child. No – the gun, my gun, wouldn't have any problems at all with getting the job done.

That sort of confidence requires an empty mind. A bottomless pit of a conscience. It would require somebody not to be human. Ironically, a gun would do just fine. It wasn't human. It was metal. Forged by the hands of a human. A human that most likely didn't give too much thought about the lives the gun may take in its tours of duty. But the time for thinking was soon up. The troop carrier was starting to rattle less as it descended toward the ground.

We were seconds away from planetary touchdown. Once the ship made contact with the foreign soil of the Tribeca planet, then the doors would open. We'd all then be expected to make our way out of the ship and onto the ground, no matter what lay in wait for us. There could be a seventy-foot-tall dinosaur waiting to munch on a bunch of Marines, and we'd still be expected to go out there with a smile on our faces.

Missions like these ended up the same way every time. We would win, but at the same time we would lose – lose many men. It was the price of war. The human body was expendable. It was just flesh and bones. And at the rate that humanity reproduced, there would never be a short supply of humans. People back on Earth sure liked to fuck. Everybody I knew had some sort of baby, or kid hanging around. Schools were filled to the brim with children eager to learn. Millions of bottles of milk every morning – making Kids grow big and strong. I didn't want kids. I didn't want more people going through what I went through in my crappy existence thus far. They tell you to get married and to start a family. To enjoy life. Go out on picnics. Chase your smiling kids down the park. Ballgames. Swimming holes. Tire swings. A cabin in the woods. That's the stuff that freedom is made out of.

But then they call you for enlistment. Man or woman, enlistment is mandatory. Two years' service – or else. That's why I'm here. Mandatory enlistment. I'll do my two years. I'll kill whoever they ask me to kill. The thing is, unlike most of the people on board this troop carrier, I won't be doing it with a smile on my face. I'll be doing it whilst gritting my teeth. I'll be doing it begrudgingly. They'll never know that I don't enjoy the prospect of spilling blood for the simple and primitive objective of financial or economic gain.

"Touchdown in thirty seconds," the Marine sergeant said while standing up and turning toward us. He gave me a wink and I smiled. It was all I could do. It just didn't feel right winking back at a grown man. I'm sure he understood my predicament.

"Things are going to get messy down here. There will be a lot of firefights. The pirates are armed to the teeth and so are the natives. Most of the fighting seems to be happening in the rock quarry fields to the east of the city. We're landing around ten clicks north of it. Once we touchdown, every one of you will make your way toward the quarry. Good luck out there and don't get killed. As my daddy used to tell me, you only get one chance at dying – might as well make it memorable. So no fuckups out there, just get the job done and get your arses back here in one piece."

The Marines around me whooped and hollered as the troop transporter shook violently. I braced myself, the railgun in my hands shaking in parallel with the transporter. My legs vibrated as the air vehicle swayed from left to right. My heart was in my mouth. I could taste copper. Iron. Blood was rushing through my head. My ears felt like cotton. I couldn't hear much. I couldn't see much more. The red light above the exits flashed rapidly. We were seconds away from touchdown. And before I knew it, the light above the door went green. Everybody unbuckled and stood up. The sound of hundreds and hundreds of guns being loaded and cocked reverberated off the tin walls that surrounded us. Then that sound was replaced by the new sound of swift moving boots making haste toward the double doors.

The darkened dimness of the air vehicle soon became engulfed in light. Natural light. The doors opened and the Marines disembarked. It didn't take long for the sound of gunfire to make its presence known. Within twenty seconds, most of the transporter was empty. I felt someone push me. I stumbled forward, my railgun still tightly in my grip. Then I craned my head back and saw who'd pushed me. It was the sergeant. He was the last one on the ship. I was second to last.

We both stepped off the ship and onto the Tribeca planet. Huge mountainous peaks surrounded us. The tips of the mountains were pointed, the sun in the sky cascaded a bright warm light across the canvas of rock above us. But time was of the essence. We couldn't afford to be standing around, staring at the natural beauty that surrounded us. This was a war zone after all.

A war zone teeming with danger around every corner. If only I knew how dangerous things were to become, then maybe I wouldn't have been standing around like an idiot waiting for the danger to find me. Instead, I would have seen it coming; I would have seen it approaching us.

"Keep your wits about you, there's plenty of areas where an ambush could potentially become a reality, so stay frosty around the corners, rookie," the Marine sergeant said as he turned toward me and gave me the thumbs up.

I was heavily distracted by the glare coming from the sun above us. Not even the mountainous peaks gave us much protection from the hot beating sun. But the sun was the least of my worries. The troop carrier behind us was empty, and dust was slowly rising around us. The dust emanated from the running boots of our fellow Marines, Marines that were far in front of us now, meaning that it was just the two of us. And two lowly human souls would be nothing more than cannon fodder for whatever was lying in wait for us out here.

"We should get a move on – I have a bad feeling about this," I said, gripping tightly onto my railgun.

I'd refrained myself from scanning the area with my red dot sight. Even though it made sense to do so, I didn't want to come across as nervous in front of my Marine Sergeant. But as I stared at him, I realized that he didn't really give a hoot about me, or how I carried myself. He was also distracted.

I didn't know what was causing the distraction, but judging by the expression on his face, at least what I could see of it through the space helmet that he was wearing, it didn't look good. Whatever was distracting him commanded and deserved every morsel of his attention. Which could only mean that whatever was distracting him was dangerous as hell.

"Sir, is there something wrong?" I asked, still holding onto my railgun tightly. But the Marine sergeant didn't even acknowledge me. He just stared off into the distance.

I was about to repeat myself again, but then I heard something rustling in the bushes. The terrain around us was scarce of life, yet where the drop ship had landed there were a few instances of greenery. Bushes thick with leaves and twigs, the perfect spot for somebody... or something - to jump out on us.

But that's not what happened, it didn't come from the bushes. It came from the shadows, shadows caused by the hulking aircraft that we'd travelled in. Whatever it was, it must have used the drop ship as cover to sneak up on us. And before a gargle could leave my windpipe, I heard the rapid sound of approaching footsteps behind us. I reacted hard and fast, turning around and aiming my railgun at whatever was behind us. But there were two of them.

And only one of them was firmly in my sights.

Then I heard a scream. Before I could open fire, I felt warm and wet blood spattering up my back and neck. I knew something had happened to the Marine Sergeant. It didn't take a rocket scientist to figure that one out. But I had the approaching footsteps to deal with. Footsteps that belonged to some sort of reptilian creature. The best way I could describe it was it being akin to a velociraptor.

It seemed to walk on its hind legs, small - yet deadly arms gently bobbing up and down as it approached me. I could see the glint and glare of the sun bouncing off its talons. I didn't know if I was going crazy, but I swear I could see chunks of flesh hanging off its razor sharp claws. But before I could give the encroaching beast a second thought, my finger automatically pressed down on the trigger of the railgun and my shoulders began to buckle under its tremendous velocity and pressure.

Huge piercing bullets smashed out of the barrel and peppered the velociraptor-like dinosaur that stood in front of me. The dino hit the deck, dust and sand billowing up into the atmosphere, momentarily encasing it in a tomb of death. But the tomb of death settled, and revealed the dead reptilian on the floor, blood seeping out of various bullet holes in its thick and leathery skin. But I didn't have time to admire my kill. Suddenly, a flash of light went off in the back of my head, reminding me that I had another reptilian enemy to deal with. And it was right behind me.

I quickly turned on my heels, momentarily checking my ammunition in the clip, noticing that I still had a hundred rounds at my disposal. A small LED screen sat just before the red dot sight, keeping me up-to-date with the vitals of my firearm. On the screen it showed that I had 100/400 rounds left. It also showed that I had one round in the chamber. The LED screen suggested that the gun was operating at optimal heat and ambience levels. There was zero chance of the gun jamming. My training was kicking in. I was able to ingest all this information within the blink of an eye. Which was useful, because when I blinked once again, I saw the bloody sight in front of me.

Lying on the floor was my former Marine Sergeant, gargling his last breath as blood sprayed out of his neck. And standing menacingly above him, on its hind legs, another velociraptor-like dinosaur. The dinosaur wasn't paying much attention to me, it was too busy gnawing and tearing at my Marine Sergeant's neck. I saw chunks of flesh being ripped and torn out of my former superiors throat. For a few seconds all I could do was stand there and gasp in horror. But then I remembered the railgun in my hands. I took aim and shot one calculated bullet into the dome of my Marine sergeant. The shot to the head put him out of his misery. He was no longer being tortured and played with by the beast that was tearing chunks out of him.

But then I recalibrated my aim, swooping the sights directly onto the dinosaur that was now staring straight at me. It hadn't noticed me before, but now it had. The fun and games were over. I'd angered it. This one looked like it enjoyed playing with its food. Like it enjoyed torturing and maiming, all for the fun of it. And I'd interrupted its fun. And judging by the look on the reptiles face, its eyes piercing hot and predatory daggers into me, I didn't have much time to react.

Before I knew it, the dino was making its way towards me. It had taken four massive strides, its scrawny and bony feet firmly crunching against the sand, leaving ominous footprints behind. But the reptile was still in my sights. And there was nothing he could do to stop the onslaught of shrapnel that was about to be unleashed on him. It was all a blur, a blur facilitated by a seemingly automatic will for survival. A will for survival that I was taking very seriously indeed.

I lit the son of a bitch up with fourteen direct hits within six seconds. Fourteen large calibre bullets pierced the dino and floored him. I stood there in shock. Within the space of a minute I'd taken down two beasts. And those two beasts were my first confirmed kills. Ever. I'd expertly taken down two savage animals. Two savage animals that had ripped my superior officer's throat out. I'd failed him. I should have been quicker on my feet. Quicker to react. But instead, all I'd been able to do was put him out of his own diabolical misery.

I hadn't been an active Marine for more than ten minutes, and I'd already witnessed a fallen comrade breathe his last breath. If I didn't get my act together soon and find my fellow Marines, then I too would be breathing my last breath. A sudden panic rose within my core, slowly creeping up my throat and seeping out of my mouth like air escaping a punctured hole in a tyre.

My lungs felt deflated, like they were collapsing. My chest ached. I felt unsteady on my feet. At any moment, it felt like I could just topple over and hit the ground. The weight of the world was crushing my shoulders, my neck was stiff and sweat was dripping down my face, drenching the interior of my space helmet, fogging up the glass and making it hard for me to see.

All I could hear was the constant rasping of my lungs as air tried to find its way inside them. But the more I tried to breathe, the less I was able to. Whatever this was, it had gripped me. It was wrapping its insidious grip around my waist, slowly squeezing the life out of me. I knew that there was no escaping this. I knew that whatever this was, was the end. I tried to scramble for my radio, hitting the PDA device on my arm, searching for the bandwidth button to open up a route of communications with whoever else was on the planet with me. I'd been deserted. I could hear gunfire in the distance, but I was too disorientated to be able to pinpoint the location of the gunfire. If I'd decided to try and trudge on in my state, God knows what would happen to me. My mind was gone. It was foggy and my ears felt like cotton. I could hear the sounds around me, but they sounded like they were a million miles away. My heart was thumping in my chest, and I tried to speak into my microphone. But nothing came out. Just a slight murmur accompanied by dried lips, cracked with dehydration.

"I... need... help...," I said, or rather, stammered. I didn't get a reply. Only static.

But the static seemed far away. Everything seemed far away. I felt like I was in a tunnel, and the light at the end of it was slowly drawing itself further and further away, morphing into a black dot and then disappearing into the darkness. I felt my knees buckling. I attempted to fight it, but it overpowered me, and I slowly but surely found myself lying face down in the dirt.

I could see the sand pressing against my helmet, the visor stopping any of it from entering my suit. For some reason, I was transfixed by the minuscule grains that made up the composition of the sand I was lying face down in. I stared at each grain and wondered profoundly if that's what I was - a grain - a minuscule object, lost within the mixture of many other grains.

That's what it felt like. The other grains of sand were the many other soldiers that had landed with me on the troop carrier. But like sand, they'd fallen through the cracks of my fingers, and escaped into the atmosphere. I had no idea where any of the other Marines were. For all I knew they could have all been dead. Maybe they were. Maybe they were facedown in the dirt just like me.

My vision was slowly getting worse. The grains of sand were going out of focus. My eyelids felt heavy, and my mouth felt dry. I tried one last time to signal someone on my radio. I fumbled in the sand, slowly dragging my arm towards me, so I could get a better look at the LED screen on my wrist unit. But before I could summon the will to operate the PDA, I felt something grab me. Hands - strong hands - grabbing at my shoulders and turning me around.

I was no longer facedown in the dirt. I was now lying on my back, staring up at the blue sky above. At first, all I could see was a shadow, a silhouette of a man. It was a silhouette that I recognised. It was human in stature. It was big and hulking. Tall and impressive. It could only be a fellow Marine.

"Hey there soldier, saw you sleeping on the job and thought that maybe you'd need a hand," the silhouette said, slowly but surely turning into a fully fledged man.

I recognised the man. He'd been my section leader back at boot camp. He was known as Grimes. And Grimes was a hard ass. He'd always ring us out for being sluggish or unprofessional. I remember hating the man back at boot camp. As far as I was concerned, he was nothing but a grump. But now, right at that moment, all I had was love for the man. I was just happy to see a familiar face.

"Sorry Sir, I got a bit sleepy," I said, standing up and trying to regain my composure. I still felt wobbly on my feet, the world was still unnaturally tilted on its axis, at least to me it was.

"You okay there, soldier? You look a little green around the gills, I wouldn't want you to puke in your spacesuit. That shit is hard to get rid of, the smell hangs around for ages. So it would be wise to tell me the truth. You feeling all right?" My section leader asked, planting a firm yet gentle hand on my shoulder and squeezing.

I think he could tell that I was a little loopy. But being a Marine was all about front. You either had the front, or you were the front. In other words, you either acted tough or were tough. And I'd like to think that I was tough. Never been good at acting. But then again this was all an act. Everybody acted as if they weren't scared. As if going to war was enjoyable. Like they looked forward to it. But there's no coming back from the dead. And there's no coming back from fear. I found that out on the troop carrier when I'd puked my guts up and got chunks all over my boots. Everybody knew right then at that very moment that I was not a good actor.

"Don't worry Sir, I'll be fine, I just need to see a few friendly faces, that's all," I said, blinking a few times as I stared at my section leader who stood in front of me.

He nodded his head, catching a glimpse of the Marine Sergeant behind me. He was so hardened that he didn't even blink. Apparently, seeing a man with his throat ripped out was just another daily occurrence for this particular section leader. Yeah, Grimes was a bad ass alright. And I was overly certain that he wasn't acting. The difference between me and him was that I was a rookie, and he was a vet. A vet that had seen plenty of action, whilst I'd just dreamed of it. But there was no more dreaming now. I was in the thick of it whether I liked it or not.

"Well, you're missing all the fun. The pirates have overtaken the quarry; they're holding some of the resources hostage. Well, you know what I mean. I think they're looking to bargain their way out of this. But the natives aren't having none of it. They want their resources and the pirates. In that order. But I gather that the pirates have a response awaiting them. So we better get a move on, before you miss all the hoopla," section leader Grimes said.

I looked at him and nodded my head. The railgun felt heavy in my grip. The barrel was weighted down, even though I'd emptied half my clip into those two dinosaurs.

"What about these foul beasts? Where have they come from?" I asked, pointing directly at the first dinosaur I'd taken out. The one that snuck up on me.

Grimes started to laugh. It was a foreign sound to me. One; I hadn't heard him laugh ever. Not even during training. Not even when one of the recruits had defecated himself whilst swinging on the monkey bars. Everybody else had found that funny. But for some reason, our friend Grimes hadn't even let out a whimper. But now, now he was laughing his ass off. I must be a funny guy. A funny guy – a bad actor – a tough Marine. What a combination. Girls, queue up, there's plenty to go around.

"What's so damn funny?" I asked, my face getting hot. I don't know if it was embarrassment or anger. Probably a combination of the two.

"Don't you know nothing about these people? The natives that is? Were you even paying attention on board the troop carrier? You know… The damn briefing… That thing we do, the meeting before the mission? You know what I'm talking about right?" Grimes asked, he was still laughing, not as loud as before, this one was more of an inward laugh, a chuckle. The sort of laugh that dies down but you can still hear the rumbling of it as it trails off.

"Yeah, I was present at the briefing, but I had other things on my mind. I'm sorry, I zoned out. Call me crazy, but I was nervous. Nervous of what war would feel like. Because I knew that this was gonna be messy. The Marine sergeant had run into me as my nerves began to get the better of me. He'd drummed into everybody that this would not be a cakewalk. Blood would be spilt. At least that's what he said. And by then, by the time those words had left his mouth, I was busy thinking and imagining what horrors lay in wait for us. I just didn't know there would be dinosaurs, that's all," I said, my face still feeling red raw.

Dropship One, now available on Kindle!

Search Luis Samways or L.D.P. Samways on the Kindle store to find nearly fifty books available to read! Kindle Unlimited readers get to read them all for free.

Thanks for reading.

☺

Printed in Great Britain
by Amazon